The Curse of the Black Cat

Nancy found herself in a small foyer surrounded by four doors marked with numbers and a fifth door that said Ladies. Murmuring voices carried from behind each of the classroom doors.

For a moment Nancy stood in front of the room labeled 4, gathering her thoughts and preparing herself for her new role as teaching assistant. What would the girls be like? she wondered.

A horrified shriek suddenly erupted from behind the closed door, cutting through Nancy's thoughts. More shrieks followed, and as Nancy stood still, listening, the classroom door burst open.

To Nancy's astonishment, a wild-looking black cat, its fur bristling, raced out of the classroom. Blocked by Nancy's legs, it reared back on its haunches, ears flat against its skull and teeth bared.

The cat growled. Nancy sucked in her breath. It was going to attack her!

Nancy Drew
Mystery Stories

Available from MINSTREL Books

NANCY DREW® 158

THE
CURSE OF THE BLACK CAT

CAROLYN KEENE

A
MINSTREL®
BOOK

Published by POCKET BOOKS
New York   London   Toronto   Sydney   Singapore

This book is a work of fiction. Names, characters, places and incidents are products of the author's imagination or are used fictitiously. Any resemblance to actual events or locales or persons living or dead is entirely coincidental.

A MINSTREL PAPERBACK *Original*

 A Minstrel Book published by
POCKET BOOKS, a division of Simon & Schuster, Inc.
1230 Avenue of the Americas, New York, NY 10020

Copyright © 2001 by Simon & Schuster, Inc.

ISBN: 0-7434-0661-3

First Minstrel Books printing January 2001

10 9 8 7 6 5 4 3 2 1

NANCY DREW, NANCY DREW MYSTERY STORIES, A MINSTREL BOOK and colophon are registered trademarks of Simon & Schuster, Inc.

Cover art by Franco Accornero

Printed in the U.S.A.

Contents

THE
CURSE OF THE BLACK CAT

1

Waverly Academy

"Nancy, shh! What's that noise?" Bess Marvin asked, peering anxiously through the kitchen window at Nancy Drew's backyard. Bess, Nancy, and George Fayne were cooking pancakes the morning after a sleepover at Nancy's house.

"Noise?" Nancy replied, staring at Bess with a puzzled frown. "I didn't hear anything." Standing the spoon up in the bowl of pancake batter, she scooted over to the window. "What did it sound like?"

Bess pressed her nose against the pane, then glanced back at her friend, her blue eyes wide with alarm. "It was this weird high-pitched howl," she explained. "Spooky—like a . . . ghost being killed."

"A ghost being killed?" George echoed, smiling

skeptically as she joined her friends at the window. "Impossible. The whole point of ghosts is that they're already dead."

Bess gave her cousin a withering look. "I know that. I'm describing what the noise sounded *like*." She added proudly, "Maybe you won't appreciate this, George, since you'd rather play sports than read a book, but I've been brushing up on the classics by reading these scary Edgar Allan Poe stories. Maybe I've just got ghosts on the brain."

George raised her eyebrows in surprise. "Reading instead of shopping, Bess?"

Bess tossed back her long blond hair and sniffed. "I love a good story," she declared. "Plus," she continued, glancing fondly at her rust-colored high-heeled boots, "I spent all my money last week on these boots, so there's no point in going to the mall till I save up."

Eighteen-year-old Nancy smiled at her two best friends' gentle teasing. Although Bess and George were cousins and very good friends, they couldn't have been more different. Dark-haired George, whose real name was Georgia, was a tomboy with a wry sense of humor, while Bess preferred shopping, eating, and daydreaming about boys.

An unearthly yowl cut through Nancy's thoughts.

"That's it!" Bess exclaimed, whirling back toward the window. "I don't care what you say, but that noise is like something from beyond the grave."

"Wild!" George said, cupping her hands against the glass.

Scanning the sunny backyard with its patches of melting snow, Nancy saw two small dark shapes leaping over the fence and disappearing into the alley beyond. Nancy grinned, flicking back her shoulder-length reddish blond hair. "You guys! That noise was a cat fight. Strays rummage for food in trash cans around our neighborhood, and they get territorial and fight."

"Cats?" Bess said, looking surprised. "Those adorable furry creatures can actually make a terrifying noise like that?" She frowned, then added, "But if they're scrounging for food, they must be starved. Aren't you tempted to adopt one, Nan?"

"Once I tried luring this huge gray cat into the house with food," Nancy admitted. "But it ran away the moment it saw me. These cats are totally wild, Bess, and kind of dangerous. I don't think they've ever had contact with humans."

"I've heard that if kittens haven't had contact with people by the time they're six weeks old, they're almost impossible to tame," George said. "I doubt these alley cats are going to be interested in making friends with people."

"Still," Bess put in, "it must be a rough life—depending on the streets of River Heights for your meals." She shot Nancy a sly look and added, "But I understand why they like Drew garbage. The scraps

3

from Hannah's meals must be a lot tastier than those from other trash cans."

Bess was referring to the Drews' housekeeper, Hannah Gruen, who had been part of the Drew family since the death of Nancy's mother when Nancy was three.

"Speaking of Hannah," Nancy said, "let's finish making these pancakes. They're Hannah's special blueberry pancake recipe."

Twenty minutes later, as the girls were clearing their plates, George glanced at the thermometer outside the kitchen window. "Wow!" she exclaimed. "It's fifty degrees. No wonder the snow is melting. Awesome day for a bike ride. Are you guys game?" After placing her dishes in the dishwasher, she marched toward the back door.

"A bike ride?" Bess said doubtfully. "I don't know, George. That sounds pretty risky for February. I mean, the weather might suddenly turn. Who knows when the next blizzard might dump two feet of snow on us?" She crossed over to her backpack, which was slung over a kitchen chair, and drew out a battered copy of a book titled *Famous American Short Stories.*

As Nancy peered curiously over her shoulder, Bess flipped through the book. At one point an illustration of a nasty-looking cat, its back arched and fur standing on end, caught Nancy's eye. But she barely had a chance to see it before Bess turned the page.

"Thanks, George, but I think I'll pass up the bike ride to go home and read," Bess announced, scanning the table of contents. "This time, though, I'll try a different writer—someone less scary."

The phone rang. Bess jumped, slapping her book closed.

"Hello?" Nancy said into the receiver.

"Nancy," a woman said briskly on the other end of the line. "This is Sarah Cook, the headmistress of Waverly Academy for Girls. I'm a friend of your father's. You and I met at one of his parties, I don't know if you remember."

"Yes, I do, Mrs. Cook," Nancy said, remembering a small, frail-looking widow with a strong personality that didn't match her looks. "Would you like to speak to Dad?"

"Actually, I'm looking for you, Nancy. Could you please come over to the school immediately?" Nancy was surprised by Mrs. Cook's nervous tone. At the party her manner had been calm and self-assured. "There's something I'd like to discuss with you."

Nancy hesitated. A bike ride with George had sounded tempting. "Could I come later today?" Nancy asked. "My friend George Fayne and I were just heading out the door with our bikes."

"I need to see you now, Nancy," Mrs. Cook said firmly. "Why don't you ride your bike over here? And by all means, bring George."

"But why do you want to see me?"

"I'll explain everything when we meet," Mrs. Cook

said. "It's ten of eleven now. I'll expect you by eleven-thirty." She hung up abruptly, without giving Nancy a chance to respond.

Nancy placed the handset back in the cradle, feeling puzzled and curious.

"It sounds as if you might have another mystery on your hands," Bess said cheerfully, after Nancy told Bess and George about her conversation. "I'll be happy to help out if you need me. Just give me a call at home."

Nancy smiled. Even though she was still a teenager, Nancy was a skilled detective. Her two best friends were used to helping her solve difficult mysteries.

"Count me in, too," George declared. "I'd love to know what Mrs. Cook wants."

Nancy headed toward the hallway to grab her coat. "Well, George, let's go find out."

At eleven twenty-five Nancy and George locked their bikes to a bike rack in front of the main building at Waverly Academy. As Nancy pocketed her key, she checked to make sure her new penlight was there.

"Dad gave this to me," she explained, showing it to George. "He thought it might come in handy."

"Well, this place looks like mystery central," George commented, gazing around.

Nancy looked up at the huge stone mansion, which served as the school's main building. A boarding school for high school girls, Waverly had an excellent academic reputation, and students came from all across the United States to go there.

"Tower, 1890" was carved in stone above the front portico. A cupola jutted from the roof above the fourth floor, with an enormous bell resting on its top. Ivy cascaded down the stone walls, and narrow Gothic windows pierced the facade like watchful eyes.

Despite the mild winter weather, Nancy shivered. She had no trouble believing that a crime might have occurred in this dark, forbidding place.

She scanned the grounds. Clumps of melting snow dotted the wide lawn, over which enormous fir trees cast dark shadows. Several smaller buildings were connected to Tower by a network of gravel paths. Except for a crow cawing in a nearby tree, Nancy and George were the only living creatures in sight.

"Do you think everyone's been abducted by aliens and we're the last people left on Earth?" George quipped.

Nancy laughed. "Let's hope they've left Mrs. Cook. I'm dying to know what she wants."

As the two girls approached Tower, a bell changed. As if on cue, the front door opened and groups of chattering girls spilled onto the portico, clutching books and backpacks. Ignoring Nancy and George, they hurried down the steps and swooped toward outlying buildings like swallows scattering in a breeze.

Nancy and George squeezed past the girls and entered Tower. Inside, a long hallway stretched before them into the depths of the building. Its walls were covered with student artwork and bulletin boards plastered with announcements and schedules.

Nancy and George glanced into a large common room on their left where tables with books and board games were set up. Two girls were frantically putting away pieces of a chess game, while a third was grabbing up stray pieces of paper to shove into her notebook binder.

Across the hall from the common room was an administrative office with the words "Mr. Moralis, School Secretary" painted on a wooden plaque above a large windowlike opening.

Nancy peered through the office window at an elderly white-haired man pecking away at an ancient typewriter set on an antique desk. Nearby, a middle-aged man and a young woman were vigorously scrolling through files at state-of-the-art computers.

"Mr. Moralis?" Nancy said.

At the sound of his name the white-haired man hopped out of his chair and hurried over to Nancy. His manner seemed much younger than his appearance, Nancy thought.

"May I help you?" he asked eagerly, his dark eyes twinkling.

"I'm Nancy Drew and this is George Fayne," Nancy said. "We're here to see Mrs. Cook."

"She's expecting you. Take the elevator just before the stairs to the fifth-floor cupola—her office."

Down the hallway the girls could see a flight of carpeted stairs leading up to a landing where a stained-glass window threw glints of colored light on the walls. Before the stairway they spotted an alcove with an oak door and an elevator button on the wall next to it.

The girls thanked Mr. Moralis, then headed for the elevator. A few straggling students trotted breathlessly past them toward the outside door.

"Hurry, girls! You're late for class," Mr. Moralis scolded, poking his head out of his office window. "It's already eleven-thirty, and the second bell's about to ring."

The stragglers broke into a run and disappeared through the front door as the second bell echoed through the building.

"What do you think happens in this place if they're late?" George asked Nancy in a low voice.

"Twenty-four hours without meals in our dankest dungeon," Mr. Moralis cut in, chuckling at his joke. "Now, girls, you'd better hurry up to Mrs. Cook. She doesn't like tardiness."

As the girls reached the elevator, Nancy noticed a cavernous dining hall at the end of the hall beyond the stairway. Double oak doors opened into a cathedral-like space, where long rectangular tables had been set for lunch.

"Let's take a quick peek at the dining room before we go up," Nancy suggested to George. "It looks awesome—like something out of a medieval monastery."

9

Just before they reached the double doors, Nancy heard a strange muffled sound.

The girls froze, listening.

"It's coming from there," Nancy whispered, pointing to a closed door off the hall before the dining room.

"A girl is crying," George said.

Low wrenching sobs carried from behind the door. Nancy felt a stab of pity. The girl sounded totally heart-broken, she thought.

She knocked on the door. There was a terrified gasp as the girl sucked in air, making a hideous rattle in her throat. Then there was silence.

2

A Cry from the Closet

"Are you all right?" Nancy called through the the door.

The silence was so complete that Nancy wondered if the girl was holding her breath. "I'd like to make sure you're okay," Nancy said.

Once more there was no response.

Turning to George, Nancy said, "I hate to barge in on her, but I'm worried she might be hurt."

"I agree," George said. "Why don't you see if the door is locked? Because if it is, I think you should alert someone. We can't just leave her locked in there and crying."

Biting her lip, Nancy twisted the doorknob and pulled. The door opened. Inside was an unlit closet filled with brooms, mops, and cleaning supplies. A small dark-haired girl wearing a diamond nose stud knelt in the center of the floor, her eyes wet and filled with dread as she stared up at Nancy and George. For a moment she stayed entirely still, like a deer frozen in headlights. But just as Nancy was about to ask if she needed help, the girl sprang to her feet and darted past Nancy and George. Casting one quick startled glance behind her, she dashed back to the staircase and pounded up the stairs.

Nancy and George traded surprised looks. Nancy realized the girl was probably embarrassed to be caught crying by two strangers, but she was too curious about the girl's predicament to let the matter drop. What if the girl really needed someone's help?

Grabbing George's arm, Nancy urged, "Let's try one more time to talk to her."

They traced the girl's steps down the hallway and up the stairs, but by the time they reached the landing with the stained-glass window, there was still no sign of her.

Taking the rest of the stairs two at a time, the girls bounded up to the second floor. Doors opened on either side of the long hall, about twenty-six of them, Nancy calculated. She peeked into the first room.

Two iron beds covered with spotless white linen bedspreads were lined up side by side on the right wall. Two bureaus painted sky blue stood opposite the beds. Books were carefully arranged inside a bookshelf between the far windows.

"Whew! These girls sure are neat. Maybe Mrs. Cook

punishes them horribly if their rooms are messy," George commented wryly.

"This one's a little messier," Nancy said, slipping into the room next door. Sweaters and books had been dumped on the bureaus and desks, while shoes cluttered the floor. But once again, two immaculate white bedspreads lay like clean snow upon the twin iron beds.

Nancy continued down the hall, casting a quick look into each room as she jogged by.

"No one's here," George said, right behind her. "They're all in class, I guess. That girl must have been playing hooky."

Nancy shrugged as she returned to the staircase. "I guess we won't find out. We seem to have lost her."

George glanced up the stairs that led to higher floors. "Let's not give up yet. If Mrs. Cook's office is in the fifth-floor cupola, I'll bet there are more dorm rooms on the third and fourth floors."

"Yes, but they'd take a while to search," Nancy remarked. "And speaking of Mrs. Cook, she's probably wondering where we are. I'm sure Mr. Moralis told her we arrived ten minutes ago."

They hurried back down the stairs. At the bottom Nancy pressed the Up button for the elevator and added, "At least we can satisfy our curiosity about one thing—in a minute we'll learn what Mrs. Cook wants."

Through a round porthole in the door, Nancy watched as the elevator descended to the first floor.

When it reached the floor, she opened the door and stepped inside with George.

The elevator cab was a tiny brass cage that looked as if it had been built at the dawn of electricity. The moment Nancy pushed the button marked "Mrs. Cook," the antique gate slammed shut and the elevator jerked slowly upward, shuddering and groaning with every inch it climbed. Just as Nancy thought the trip would never end, the elevator lurched to a stop and the gate clanked open.

Nancy and George stepped directly from the elevator into a large octagonal office under the bell tower. With its bright oriental rug, comfortable armchairs, and fire in the grate, the room was cheerful and cosy.

Behind an enormous mahogany desk sat a diminutive gray-haired woman wearing large wire-rimmed spectacles. Nancy immediately recognized Mrs. Cook— tiny but formidable.

"Where have you been, girls?" Mrs. Cook asked in a no-nonsense tone, not waiting for an answer. "It's past eleven-thirty. Please, take a seat—let's not waste any more time." She motioned them to the two armchairs in front of her desk.

Sitting down, Nancy and George looked respectfully across the desk at the headmistress and waited for her to speak.

"Let me get straight to the point," Mrs. Cook went on as she pushed aside some papers and leaned in toward the girls. "We've had a couple of strange incidents here recently, and I'm hoping that you can get to the bottom of these problems, Nancy."

"What kind of incidents?" Nancy asked.

"I'd rather not explain, until you let me know if you'd be interested in solving this case—with George as your assistant, of course." Mrs. Cook flashed George a brief smile. "You see, Waverly Academy has a spotless reputation, and I don't want too many people to know about our problems. If you're not interested in helping, I'll simply ask someone else."

Nancy frowned. How could she agree to help Mrs. Cook without knowing the exact problem? What if they were so bad that Mrs. Cook was afraid no detective would want to take on the case? Nancy didn't want to be roped into agreeing to help and then regret her decision.

Still, she was curious to know more.

"Can't you give me a little more information, Mrs. Cook?" Nancy asked. "I'd at least like to figure out whether I'm the right person for this case."

Mrs. Cook smiled, her silvery eyes lighting up behind her glasses. "I have no doubt you're the right person, Nancy. I've heard quite a bit about your detective skills from your father. I've also heard that your friends Bess and George are valuable helpers. You're the perfect person for the job."

"Thank you, Mrs. Cook, but I still don't think I can take on any case blindly," Nancy said.

"Then allow me to explain what your jobs at Waverly

15

would be," Mrs. Cook went on, without missing a beat. "You could both go undercover here by posing as teaching interns. Sometimes we allow college students who are getting their teaching degrees to do their student teaching here. The students are familiar with that setup. They wouldn't find anything suspicious about your position."

"Would I actually have to do some teaching?" Nancy asked.

"That depends upon the teacher to whom I assign you. You would be in the classroom to help the teacher in any way he or she felt necessary. Whenever you weren't in class, you'd be free to investigate." Mrs. Cook took off her spectacles and rubbed her eyes wearily, then added, "A teaching intern is part of the Waverly community. Life would go on here as usual. The person who's responsible for these incidents wouldn't know that you're really a detective and would be off guard around you. That should make the culprit much easier to catch."

Nancy glanced at George, who sneaked her a thumbs-up sign.

A bell rang. "Lunch period," Mrs. Cook said briskly. "Now, ladies, I'm determined to find out who is behind this mischief before anyone gets hurt—and also before our excellent reputation suffers. Today is Tuesday, and I'd like to wrap up this matter by Thursday at noon when we close for Midwinter Weekend. So tell me, are you on board, or not?"

Before Nancy could answer, the phone on Mrs. Cook's desk rang. "Mrs. Cook," the headmistress answered, picking it up.

After a brief pause Mrs. Cook went on, "Send her up, please, Mr. Moralis," and then hung up the phone. She looked sharply at Nancy and George. "Saved by the bell. You two have just been granted a few more minutes to think about your answer. I'm sorry if I've been secretive about this matter, but I must always consider what's best for the school."

The elevator door burst open, and a dark-haired girl stumbled into the office. Nancy caught her breath, trading a surprised look with George. It was the girl who had been crying in the broom closet earlier.

Wild-eyed, the girl trembled from head to toe. Holding a piece of paper in her outstretched hand, she wailed, "It's the Black Cat, Mrs. Cook. I've been cursed!"

3

Cat Attack

Mrs. Cook's face went ashen. "Not again!" she cried, shooting out of her chair. She hurried around her desk to comfort the girl.

With her entire body shaking, the girl broke into fresh sobs as Mrs. Cook put an arm around her shoulders. "Now, now, Sindu. Everything's okay," Mrs. Cook crooned, leading the girl toward a nearby chair. "You've had a nasty experience, but you're all right. Now let me see this note."

As soon as she settled Sindu into the chair, Mrs. Cook gently pried the paper from the girl's hand and returned to her desk to read it.

For the first time since she'd entered the room, Sindu made eye contact with Nancy and George. A

18

quiver of alarm went through her as she recognized them, and she looked as if she might bolt from the room.

Mrs. Cook seemed sensitive to the girl's fears. "Don't let my guests disturb you, my dear," she said. "They'll keep this matter entirely confidential. Sindu, please meet Nancy Drew, our new English intern working under Ms. Friedlander, and George Fayne, our new sports intern assisting Ms. Kahn."

Nancy and George exchanged looks of complete astonishment. Nancy tried to catch Mrs. Cook's eye, but the headmistress ignored her as she went on, "Nancy and George, allow me to introduce Sindu Bannerjee, a ninth grader."

"It's nice to meet you both," Sindu said meekly, trying to manage a smile.

"And it's nice to meet you, too," Nancy said, while George smiled warmly at Sindu.

"Sindu, dear," Mrs. Cook began as she examined Sindu's note, "tell me exactly what happened before you received this note."

Sindu tucked her chin down, looking shy and embarrassed. "Well, uh . . . let me see," she stammered. "It all began with Ramona Lopez's birthday present."

"What about Ramona's present?" Mrs. Cook prompted.

"Well, see, I bought her this really cool CD. Oh, it's so hard to explain!" Sindu exclaimed, flustered.

"Just try," Mrs. Cook said encouragingly.

Sindu studied her lap, her cheeks flushed. "I . . . I haven't made all that many friends at Waverly," she began. "I'm kind of shy, and I don't always know what to say to people. But Ramona is the most popular girl in the ninth grade. She always knows exactly what to say to get people to like her—she and her cliquey friends."

"But you've got other qualities, dear, like your considerable intelligence," Mrs. Cook said soothingly. "You've earned a perfect score on every math test you've taken here, and your English essay recently won a prize."

"I'm happy about my studies," Sindu said, "but what I'd love more than anything is to be popular and cool. So I bought Ramona this CD by this awesomely hot group called Wilderness. . . ." She paused, her lip trembling.

"Hoping to make a good impression on Ramona and her friends," Mrs. Cook finished with a sigh. When Sindu shot her a surprised look, Mrs. Cook went on, "I'm not as out-of-it as some of you girls might think, dear. I was in high school once, too, you know, and I see what goes on here."

"So then what happened?" Nancy asked Sindu. "Ramona didn't like her CD?"

"It's not that," Sindu said, throwing up her hands in frustration. "When Ramona opened my present this morning, there was a different CD inside. It was a group called the Black Cats, who are beyond out!"

Sindu's eyes moistened, and she bit her lip to hold

back her tears. Drawing a ragged breath, she murmured, "When they saw the CD, Ramona and her friends all giggled. Then one of them tossed it aside. Then, when I tried to explain, they ignored me, and now things are worse than ever."

"Sindu," Nancy said gently, "is that why you were crying when we saw you earlier?"

Without meeting Nancy's eyes, Sindu nodded.

"After you ran off, George and I tried to find you," Nancy said. "We wanted to make sure you were okay."

"Thanks," Sindu said, swiping at her eyes. "I ran back to my room on the fourth floor. I didn't mean to be rude, but I couldn't face anyone. At least it was a free period for me."

"Let's get back to the note, Sindu," Mrs. Cook said. "Did you receive it after you gave Ramona the present?"

"Not immediately," Sindu replied. "Ramona got her presents in the common room, and afterward I was so upset that I hid out downstairs for a few minutes before running back to my room." She caught Nancy's eye and continued, "In my room I found an envelope on my bureau with my name typed on it. The note was inside."

"I see," Mrs. Cook said. "And you're sure the envelope wasn't there earlier?"

"I would have seen it when I was getting dressed this morning—it definitely wasn't there."

"I want you to go to lunch now, Sindu—the period's almost over." Mrs. Cook added gravely, "Even though you're all right and I'm sure nothing else will happen to you, please be on your guard today. I can assure you that school officials will be investigating the incident."

Sindu rose from her chair and thanked Mrs. Cook. Once the elevator gate clanked shut behind her, Mrs. Cook said, "Well, ladies, I might as well tell you what's been going on at Waverly. But please give me your word that you won't tell anyone outside the school community about our problems if you decide not to take on the investigation."

"You'll have a lot of explaining to do to Sindu if we say no," George commented dryly.

Mrs. Cook smiled and said, "Even though I told Sindu you were interns, I'm sure you realize that I can't force you to work here. But I *was* hoping that my words might influence you to come on board."

Nancy leaned forward, eager to hear about the other incidents and to know what was in Sindu's letter, and said, "We promise not to tell anyone outside the school what's happened here, even if we don't take on the case."

"Except for our friend Bess," George chimed in.

"That is all right with me," Mrs. Cook said, smiling. "Now let me fill you in. What happened to Sindu is the third incident. The first one happened yesterday when the captain of the basketball team, Lucy Slingluff, was about to compete in a big game against a rival school. But when Lucy went to the locker room to change, she found the soles of her sneakers covered with tar. They were her lucky pair, which she always wears for big games. Needless to say, they were ruined."

"The person broke into her locker to get to the sneakers?" Nancy asked.

"Someone must have found the key because the locker door wasn't open," Mrs. Cook explained. "Anyway, Lucy found an envelope with her first name on it tucked inside her shoe. There was a curse note inside."

"What was the second incident?" George asked.

"That happened early this morning," Mrs. Cook said. "One of our seniors, Eliza McBride, is a lead in the school play, which is running for two nights, today and tomorrow. The play is *Camelot*, and Eliza plays Guinevere. When the play was cast, the director specifically wanted a long-haired girl to play the part. Eliza has—or should I say had?—beautiful long golden hair, perfect for the part. But when she woke up this morning, she found all of it lying at the foot of her bed, completely cut off before opening night!"

"Whoa!" George said. "So someone sneaked into her room during the night and cut off her hair while she was sleeping?"

"Just as with Samson and Delilah," Mrs. Cook said, nodding.

"Did Eliza get a curse note?" Nancy asked.

"A note was taped to her bed," Mrs. Cook said, "and Eliza, being the dramatic type, instantly spread the news around the school. She's not a person to curb her feelings, and believe me, she made no secret of her complaints."

"Well, it *would* be a shock to wake up to a surprise haircut," George said.

"I don't mean to sound unsympathetic, but what happened to Sindu was crueler," Mrs. Cook said. "Eliza loves attention, even if she had to sacrifice her own hair to get it. Anyway, my point is that Eliza's story went around the school like wildfire. All the girls—and the teachers—were extremely upset. That's when I called you, Nancy."

"I see," Nancy said. "Could I see the curse notes?"

Mrs. Cook handed Sindu's note to Nancy. Then, after rummaging in her desk, she brought out two more. Nancy spread them out side by side on the front of the desk to compare them. All three looked exactly the same. On a sheet of white paper, the words "The Black Cat curses you until the day you die!" stood out starkly in black computer print.

But what sent a shiver through Nancy was the illustration of a black cat, with eyes painted red and sharp vampire teeth.

Nancy frowned, trying to jog her memory. There was something familiar about the picture.

She ran a finger over the image. Except for the painted eyes, it was made from an ink stamp, she saw.

Nancy chewed her lip. Who could be putting curses on the girls at Waverly? she wondered. And why?

Meeting Mrs. Cook's hopeful gaze, Nancy said, "I'd be happy to take on the case, Mrs. Cook."

"And I'm here to help, too," George added.

"Excellent!" Mrs. Cook exclaimed, beaming. "Then let's get down to business." She glanced at a wall clock. "How the time has flown! We're already into the first period after lunch. Nancy, you're to report to Angela Friedlander's sophomore English class. The English department is in a white clapboard cottage to the right of Tower. It's called 'Shakespeare.' Her class is in Room Four. George, please join the sports teacher, Zoe Kahn, in the gym. I believe she's coaching junior varsity basketball practice. And please," she added, "report the slightest suspicions or problems that you have to me. I want up-to-the-minute details on this troubling situation."

Nancy and George promised Mrs. Cook that they'd keep her closely informed.

Once outside, the two girls parted ways. Nancy followed a gravel path that curved around the right side of Tower toward a small white house with green shutters. The name "Shakespeare" appeared in green script on a wooden plaque above the door.

Inside, Nancy found herself in a small foyer surrounded by four doors marked with numbers and a fifth door that said Ladies. Murmuring voices carried from behind each of the classroom doors.

Nancy stood in front of the room labeled 4 for a moment, gathering her thoughts and preparing herself for her new job. What would the girls be like? she wondered. Would they be easy to get along with or difficult? All of a sudden, hang gliding or scuba diving seemed easy compared to facing a classroom full of tenth graders, she thought grimly.

A horrified shriek suddenly erupted from behind the closed door, cutting through Nancy's thoughts. More shrieks followed, and as Nancy stood still, listening, the classroom door burst open.

To Nancy's astonishment, a huge, wild-looking black cat, its fur bristling, raced out of the classroom. Blocked by Nancy's legs, it reared back on its haunches, ears flat against its skull and teeth bared.

The cat growled. Nancy sucked in her breath. It was going to attack her!

4

Nancy's Special Welcome

Nancy jumped aside. The cat shot past her and sprang through an open window in the hall.

Before Nancy could collect her thoughts, a dark-haired woman in her twenties burst out of the classroom, followed by several excited girls. The woman wore horn-rimmed glasses, red lipstick, and a narrowly cut black skirt.

Nancy noticed the woman's hands, which had a couple of welts on them.

"Catastrophe!" the woman yelled, almost colliding with Nancy. She stopped short, eyeing Nancy suspiciously.

"Are you Ms. Friedlander?" Nancy asked.

"I am," the teacher replied formally.

"I'm Nancy Drew. Mrs. Cook has just hired me as a teaching intern. She assigned me to your class."

Ms. Friedlander's attractive face brightened. "Fabulous!" she exclaimed. "Mrs. Cook told me this morning she was thinking of hiring a student teacher to help me out. She certainly acts quickly."

"Let's put something on those welts," Nancy offered.

Ms. Friedlander glanced down at her hands and winced. "There's a first-aid kit in the bathroom." She turned back to her class and said, "The cat has gone, girls, and everything's okay. I'm going to take care of my hands. In the meantime, please sit down quietly and study for your test."

Nancy followed Ms. Friedlander to the bathroom in case she needed help. Once there, Ms. Friedlander pulled a first-aid kit out of a cabinet.

"You couldn't have come at a better time, Nancy," Ms. Friedlander said, sifting through the contents for some salve. "As you've no doubt noticed, it's been nuts around here."

As Ms. Friedlander washed her hands and arm in soothing cold water, Nancy asked her what had happened.

"I was getting ready to give my class a quiz on 'The Black Cat' by Edgar Allan Poe," she explained. "I needed to hand out exam booklets, which were in the big drawer at the bottom of my desk. But the moment I opened the drawer, a real black cat leaped out of it! I can't describe to you my astonishment."

"I would think the cat would have meowed if he'd been shut up in a drawer," Nancy remarked.

Ms. Friedlander shrugged. "Maybe the drawer had been open earlier and he'd crawled inside to sleep. Someone could have shut it without seeing him. He'd probably been sleeping there up to the moment I woke him."

"I guess that's the only explanation," Nancy said as she applied salve to Ms. Friedlander's welts. "But isn't it kind of a coincidence that a black cat shows up on the same day you're giving an exam on the subject?"

"Not really," Ms. Friedlander said. "That cat is a familiar presence at this school. We call him Catastrophe, nickname Tassie, and he's always lurking around, even when we aren't reading 'The Black Cat.' His name says it all."

"Who does he belong to?" Nancy asked.

"He's a stray, and he's so wild that no one can touch him. That's why he attacked me when I tried putting him out the door. I'm lucky he didn't break my skin. But I had to get him out. He was jumping on desks and scaring the girls."

"He was probably terrified himself," Nancy said.

"I just wish he'd go away," Ms. Friedlander said. "But I suspect that someone around here sneaks him food—probably a tenderhearted student."

"Has he ever attacked anyone before?" Nancy asked.

"No," Ms. Friedlander said. "Mrs. Cook wouldn't tolerate that. He'd have to go to the Humane Society."

Poor Catastrophe, Nancy thought. She hoped for his sake that he'd keep out of trouble. But she couldn't help wondering—simply because he *was* a black cat—whether the curse notes had something to do with him. In that case, trouble for the cat might have only just begun.

"By the way," Nancy said, "have you heard about the curse notes?"

Ms. Friedlander frowned. "I heard about them earlier. Two students had tricks played on them and then received these threatening notes."

"Three students, now," Nancy said.

"Really?" Ms. Friedlander said, her face clouding with concern. "How dreadful!"

"I'm just wondering if Tassie turning up in your drawer wasn't a deliberate trick. Are you sure there wasn't a curse note nearby?" Nancy asked.

Ms. Friedlander looked puzzled. "Not that I noticed. But he jumped out so fast—I wasn't paying attention to anything else. Let's go take a look around the desk."

After putting away the first-aid kit, Ms. Friedlander led the way back to the classroom. Inside, a few girls were giggling and passing notes while others were studying quietly. But the instant Ms. Friedlander crossed the threshhold, the class hushed.

"That's better!" Ms. Friedlander declared, fixing the girls who had been talking with a pointed stare.

Skirting the girls' desks, Nancy and Ms. Friedlander hurried to the teacher's desk at the front of the room.

The drawer where Tassie had been lying was still open. As she gazed into it, Nancy's heart skipped a beat. Right on top of a pile of exam booklets was an envelope marked "Angela."

Ms. Friedlander drew a quick breath. Then she reached down, pulled out the envelope, and tore it open with trembling hands.

As Ms. Friedlander placed it on her desk, Nancy saw that the note was exactly like the others. She peered at it closely. In a flash she remembered where she'd seen that image of the black cat—in Bess's book of American short stories. Except for the red eyes and vampire teeth, which had been added, the cat looked exactly the same.

Ms. Friedlander slumped down in her chair, staring at the note as if she'd received an electric shock. "Who could have done this?" she asked, staring blankly at Nancy.

"Did you notice anyone hanging around your classroom who didn't belong here?" Nancy asked.

"No, but we had lunch period before class. Someone could have sneaked in while we were eating. I'll ask the other English teachers if they noticed anyone suspicious."

While Nancy and Ms. Friedlander were discussing the curse note, total silence had fallen over the room—and not only because the girls were studying. The students were hanging on every word of their conversation, Nancy realized. News of Ms. Friedlander's note will be around the school the moment class lets out, she thought grimly.

Ms. Friedlander stood up abruptly. "I'm canceling class for the day," she announced to her students. "As I'm sure you've overheard, I just received a curse note, and I need to discuss it with Mrs. Cook. I'd like you all to go to the library and study. I'm postponing the test until tomorrow."

The classroom erupted into a cacophony of voices as the girls collected their books and left. Some students acted thrilled to be let out of class, while others seemed troubled that yet another prank had happened at their once safe school.

As soon as Ms. Friedlander had gone, Nancy searched the classroom for clues, but there was no sign of anything unusual. Opening the top drawer of the desk, Nancy picked up a copy of the book the students had been reading while they'd waited for Ms. Friedlander to see to her hands. It was a paperback titled *Edgar Allan Poe's Collected Works*. Unlike Bess's book, it had no illustrations.

Nancy put away the book, then headed for the gym

to tell George about the new curse note. As she walked down the gravel path, the balmy air seemed springlike, she mused. It was hard to believe that someone evil was at work in this peaceful place.

Nancy found George helping a fit-looking woman with a long dark ponytail coach a basketball game in the gym.

"Hi, Nancy, what's up?" George said, taking time out from the game to jog over to her.

Nancy told George about Ms. Friedlander's encounter with Catastrophe. "When you finish with your class, George," she added, "let's go to my house for lunch. We missed it here, and I'm starved. Plus, I want to call Bess and get another look at her book. There's an illustration in it that reminds me of the cat on the curse notes."

"Okay," George said. "Bess will want to know what's happening."

"I know," Nancy said. "As soon as the bell rings, we'll go."

Ten minutes later Nancy and George stopped at Tower to leave a note for Mrs. Cook to explain what they were doing. As they went outside and approached the bike rack, Nancy noticed something white stuck in the spokes of her wheel.

It was an envelope, with her first name printed on it. Nancy and George exchanged looks. Nancy's hands shook as she opened it. There was no doubt in her mind about what was inside.

Even though she had prepared herself for the ugly threat, a shiver of horror ran through her as she stared at the note. It was exactly the same as the others, except for a P.S. in block letters at the bottom.

"Back off, Nancy Drew," it said, "or the Black Cat will curse you double!"

5

No Way Out

Nancy glanced around. The next class period had already started, and the school grounds were deserted.

"There's no one in sight," George said uneasily as Nancy stuck the note in her coat pocket. "Shouldn't we tell Mrs. Cook about this?"

"We'll tell her when we get back," Nancy said. "I'm in a hurry to check out Bess's book."

The girls hopped on their bikes and started down Waverly's long drive. The breeze, which was tossing the boughs of the fir trees, had a sudden cool edge, and Nancy hunched forward to protect herself against it.

Nancy couldn't shake off her chill, though, which she realized was not caused by the wind. Pranks happened to all the other people who had received notes,

35

and she doubted she'd be an exception. She only wondered what kind of prank would be played on her.

Once the girls reached Nancy's house, they found Hannah in the kitchen, throwing handfuls of noodles into a large pot on the stove.

Hannah beamed when she saw them. "You're just in time for a bowl of my turkey noodle soup, girls," she announced. "It'll be ready in a couple of minutes. In the meantime, can I make you sandwiches? There's some turkey left, and homemade peanut butter, too."

"Peanut butter and jelly sounds great, Hannah," Nancy said, brightening. "Thanks."

"And I'll go for turkey, please, Hannah," George said. "But let me help—you're busy."

While Hannah and George prepared lunch, Nancy called Bess and filled her in on the case.

"I'll be over right away with my book," Bess promised before hanging up.

Fifteen minutes later Nancy and George were finishing lunch when Bess walked in the door. She tossed a book on the kitchen table in front of Nancy.

"Thanks, Bess," Nancy said, picking up the book. Nancy turned to the copyright page and saw that the book, *Famous American Short Stories,* was almost seventy years old. She doubted there were many other copies of it around.

"I bought that book in a used bookstore a few weeks

ago," Bess told her, after Nancy had asked her where she'd found it.

"Now, let's see if these two cats are the same," Nancy said, spreading out the curse note next to her on the table. She turned to the first page of "The Black Cat" in Bess's book.

"Whoa!" she said, gaping at the image. Except for the painted eyes and teeth, the cats were identical.

"Bingo!" George exclaimed as she and Bess peered at the images over Nancy's shoulder. "Here's our first clue. Whoever sent these notes must have copied this cat to make their stamp. So if we can just find someone at Waverly who owns this book—or this stamp—we're in luck."

"But how many students go to Waverly, anyway?" Bess asked, frowning. "You guys will have to sneak into tons of rooms to look for that book. It's kind of like locating a needle in a haystack. And what if the book is assigned reading for a course? Then lots of girls will have it."

"The edition is too old for that," Nancy said, clearing her lunch dishes. "I think when we get back to school, we should talk to Mrs. Cook, and try to narrow down some suspects. At that point we can search their rooms."

Nancy and George said goodbye to Hannah and Bess, then drove in Nancy's Mustang back to school. Once there, they saw a throng of girls streaming into the auditorium.

"Mrs. Cook called a special assembly," a girl told Nancy when Nancy asked her what was happening.

"She wants to talk to the whole school, including faculty."

"Why?" Nancy asked uneasily.

The girl shrugged. "Beats me," she said, and ran ahead to join some friends.

Nancy and George took seats with the rest of the faculty in the front two rows.

Seconds later Mrs. Cook strode purposefully on to the stage and stood beside the podium, which was almost the same size she was. An immediate hush fell over the room.

"I'm sure everyone can guess why we're here," Mrs. Cook said in her strong, clear voice. "I'd like to discuss this dreadful matter of the curse notes and answer any questions you may have, before rumors start to fly. I also want you girls to know that I still consider Waverly Academy to be a safe place. The administration is doing its best to find—and punish—the guilty person."

Without embarrassing Sindu by giving out too many details of her curse, Mrs. Cook described each of the curses and then finished by saying, "Even though I urge everyone to stay calm, I expect you ladies to be alert and report any suspicious activity to a teacher or administrator immediately. And other than telling your parents, please don't discuss this matter outside the Waverly community." Looking at Nancy and George, she added, "I also want to introduce our new teaching

38

interns, Nancy Drew, who will be helping Ms. Friedlander, and George Fayne, who will assist Ms. Kahn."

Nancy and George stood up and nodded to the students. As they sat down again, a bell rang, and Mrs. Cook ended the assembly. Nancy threaded her way to Mrs. Cook as she came off the stage and told her about her curse note.

Mrs. Cook frowned. "So nothing bad has happened to you yet? Maybe the person's forgotten about you."

Nancy doubted she'd be so lucky, but she kept her thoughts to herself. Mrs. Cook went on, "The last academic period of the day is about to begin, Nancy. Angela Friedlander is teaching a course called Animals in Literature to interested juniors and seniors. Why don't you join her? I'm sure she'd appreciate the help."

"I'd be happy to," Nancy said. After saying goodbye to George and Mrs. Cook, she headed over to Shakespeare. Once there, Nancy found Ms. Friedlander at her desk reviewing notes while students filed into her room.

Ms. Friedlander's face lit up when she saw Nancy. "I need help grading papers," she said, "so please sit down, listen, and take notes—anything that will help you with the papers."

Nancy pulled a small desk up to Ms. Friedlander's large one and sat down. She whipped a notepad and pen out of her backpack and prepared to write.

Once the bell had rung and the students were seated, Ms. Friedlander moved to the front of her desk with a paperback book in her hands. The students—fifteen in all, Nancy counted—looked expectantly at her.

"First, I'd like to introduce Ms. Drew," Ms. Friedlander said. "She's an intern who will be helping out in my classroom." After Nancy acknowledged the class with a friendly wave, Ms. Friedlander announced, "We're going to talk about *The Jungle Book* by Rudyard Kipling now. Did everyone finish it?"

The class nodded, except for one dark-eyed girl who immediately raised her hand. "Yes, Francesca?" Ms. Friedlander said.

"I didn't finish it," Francesca proclaimed, with a slight foreign accent that Nancy couldn't place.

"Indeed?" Ms. Friedlander said icily. "And may I ask why not?"

The girl wrinkled her nose like a confused rabbit. For a moment Nancy thought she wasn't going to respond. But in a wispy voice that Nancy could barely hear, she finally said, "I've been upset about these curse notes. And when I discovered that a cat might be involved, I couldn't read anything that reminded me of cats—especially fierce ones like the tigers and panthers in *The Jungle Book.*"

Ms. Friedlander gaped at Francesca in disbelief. Then she narrowed her eyes angrily and said, "All year long you have given me excuse after excuse for not completing your assignments. But this excuse takes the cake. It's beyond silly and completely unworthy of a

Waverly student. If you don't come into class tomorrow fully prepared, I'm sending you to Detention the moment class is over."

Francesca cocked her head and gazed at Ms. Friedlander, reminding Nancy of a curious bird. She didn't seem to care that she was in trouble, Nancy thought. She seemed more interested in looping her long, black hair into a pink scrunchie than in the seriousness of Ms. Friedlander's threat.

"Did you hear me?" Ms. Friedlander said, gritting her teeth.

"Yes," Francesca said airily.

Ms. Friedlander looked over the rim of her glasses at Francesca. "May I remind you, young lady, that this class, Animals in Literature, is an elective? I can't understand why you signed up for it if you don't want to do the work."

"I'm here because I love animals," Francesca replied.

A girl with short honey-colored hair raised her hand. Her wide clear green eyes snapped with confidence, and her perfectly smooth complexion glowed, Nancy thought.

"Yes, Eliza," Ms. Friedlander said with a hint of exasperation.

"I just wanted you to know that Francesca's lying!" Eliza declared. "She's not afraid of cats—especially fierce ones. Everyone knows she sneaks food to Tassie in the school custodian's toolshed—"

"Enough!" Ms. Friedlander cut in. "If I had wanted your two cents' worth about this matter, Eliza, I'd have asked for it. Now let's get back to *The Jungle Book*."

"Please, one more thing—it's important," Eliza sputtered, ignoring Ms. Friedlander's stern look. "Since Francesca is the only person at school who's tamed Tassie, isn't it obvious that *she* must have put him in your desk earlier? Francesca's guilty, Ms. Friedlander. Only *she* could have written the notes."

"Eliza!" Ms. Friedlander warned.

"She's the one who cut off my hair!" Eliza wailed, covering her head with her hands.

"That's enough, Eliza McBride!" Ms. Friedlander said furiously. "You mustn't say such crazy things— even as a joke. How dare you accuse a classmate in front of others? If you have suspicions—and evidence, of course—take them privately to Mrs. Cook. If you say one more word about Francesca, I'm sending *you* to Detention. I'm astonished by your behavior."

When Ms. Friedlander stopped talking, the room was so quiet that Nancy could hear a buzz of voices from the class next door seeping through the walls.

"Now, can we get down to business, class?" Ms. Friedlander asked. "Who would like to talk about the different animal characters in *The Jungle Book*?"

As the girls talked about characters and themes in *The Jungle Book*, Nancy took notes, all the time observing both Eliza and Francesca. Why had Eliza been so quick to accuse Francesca? Nancy wondered. And was Eliza telling the truth when she said that only Francesca could touch Catastrophe?

Forty minutes later the next bell rang. Noise broke out as students jumped up, grabbed their books, and headed out the door. Eliza threw Ms. Friedlander a dirty look as the teacher reminded her and Francesca to behave unless they wanted to visit Detention. "And Rosie Tsing," Ms. Friedlander continued, directing her words to a stocky girl with short dark hair and glasses, "I'd like a word with you now, please."

Rosie's face hardened as Ms. Friedlander spoke to her in hushed tones. Nancy strained to listen to their conversation as she gathered up her notes. But as the last student left the classroom, Nancy felt as if she should leave, too. Otherwise, she'd seem too nosy.

Nancy decided to ask Mrs. Cook about Eliza and Francesca. She was curious to know more about them.

As she hurried toward Tower, Nancy realized that several hours had passed since she'd received her note but no actual curse had happened to her. Maybe the person *has* forgotten about me, she thought hopefully.

Inside Tower, Mr. Moralis told Nancy that Mrs. Cook wasn't in her office and that he was running out on a quick errand. "I'm sure she'll be back soon," he assured her. "Why don't you sit in the common room and keep a lookout for her?"

Peeking into the common room, Nancy found

George in an armchair, reading. "Nancy!" George said, putting down her book. "How about a game of chess?"

"Sure," Nancy said, wishing she could talk to George about the case so far. But with other students reading and playing games around them, they had to be discreet.

Twenty minutes into their chess game, Mr. Moralis handed Nancy an envelope addressed to her. "I just got back from my errand and found this in your mail cubby," he explained. "Looks like it's from Her Royal Highness," he added, chuckling.

Nancy tore open the envelope, which was engraved with Mrs. Cook's name above the return address of the school. "Please come see me right away, Nancy," the headmistress wrote. "I'm in my office."

"I'll be back in a minute, George," Nancy said.

"No hurry," George moaned. "I need time to get out of this check you put me in, anyway."

Nancy left George studying the chessboard and walked down the hall to the elevator. Opening the door, she stepped inside and pushed the button to Mrs. Cook's office. The gate slammed shut, and the elevator creaked upward.

I could spend my whole life in this thing, Nancy thought, biting her lip impatiently as the elevator crept upward at a snail's pace. Its circular window slowly beamed light from each floor she passed.

Just as Nancy thought she must be approaching the

fifth floor, the elevator gave a strange shudder. Then, with a terrifying lurch, it jerked to a stop.

Without warning, the elevator lights went out, plunging the cab into darkness.

Nancy groped for the alarm, but it was too dark to see the buttons. Even so, she punched every button she touched.

Nancy's heart sank. The alarm hadn't gone off.

Nancy was willing herself to stay calm in the black coffinlike space when she heard a noise above her.

It was a sawing noise—metal on metal. Someone was trying to cut the cable!

6

Terror Takes a Bow

The elevator gave a sickening dip. Nancy's stomach churned. Perspiration broke out on her brow from the sudden warmth of the cab and from fear. The air was stuffy and hard to breath.

I've got to get out of here, Nancy thought. But how?

She took a deep breath. "Help!" she cried as loudly as she could, hoping Mrs. Cook would hear her. "Mrs. Cook, help! It's me, Nancy."

The elevator swayed as the sawing continued. Just a few more minutes, Nancy thought, and this thing's going to crash!

Footsteps clicked rapidly somewhere nearby. A spark of hope shot through Nancy. There was no doubt that someone was coming, as the sound of determined footsteps echoed up through the shaftway wall. But is this person coming to help me or hurt me? she wondered tensely.

The sawing stopped. Footsteps thudded above her. She heard a creaking noise.

Nancy held her breath, listening to all the different sounds to try to figure out what they meant. After a moment she heard a key turn in the elevator lock and the door opened, and then a voice floated down to her through the elevator shaft. Nancy exhaled with relief. It was Mrs. Cook.

"Nancy, are you there?" she called.

"Yes!" Nancy yelled back. "The elevator's stuck."

"One minute, dear. Please bear with me."

Nancy heard a shaftway door slam shut above her. That same instant the elevator light blinked on and the elevator started rising. Seconds later it cruised smoothly to a stop at Mrs. Cook's door.

The gate opened, and Nancy pushed on the door, delighted to be free—only to find Mrs. Cook staring at her gravely.

"This situation is getting more serious by the hour," Mrs. Cook declared as Nancy stepped into her office. "What happened to you was no prank, Nancy. Our Black Cat was out to kill you."

Nancy slumped into an armchair. "You're right," she agreed. "But that doesn't mean things are getting worse for everybody. The Black Cat knows I'm investigating the case and wants me out of the way."

Mrs. Cook frowned. "I wish I could be certain that no one will be injured."

"So tell me what happened," Nancy said. "Those were your footsteps I heard coming up the stairs, right?"

"Right," Mrs. Cook replied. "I was downstairs for a good five minutes, trying to summon the elevator. It wouldn't come, so I concluded that it wasn't working and I'd better walk. Halfway up the stairs, I heard you calling me for help."

"I'm so glad you heard me!" Nancy exclaimed.

"The elevator shaftway is next to the stairway wall," Mrs. Cook explained, nodding toward the elevator and stairway doors which were located side by side. "Luckily, your voice carried through the wall. The moment I heard you, I hurried the rest of the way up the stairs. But just as I was unlocking the stairway door to my office, I heard footsteps run across my floor."

"What did they sound like?" Nancy asked.

The headmistress puckered her brow. "I'm not sure. I was so anxious to get inside to help you that all I could think of was opening my door."

"So you never actually saw anyone?" Nancy asked.

Mrs. Cook sighed. "Unfortunately, the stairway lock is difficult and requires some jiggling—I hardly ever use that door. Anyway, when I finally got in, I saw no one—only a rope dangling from an open window. By the time I stuck my head out, the intruder had disappeared."

"Hmm. Sneaking out by a fifth-floor window is pretty gutsy. I wonder if the person came in that way."

"I doubt it," Mrs. Cook said. "He or she probably knew I wasn't in and simply took the elevator up. I hardly ever lock my elevator door. Also, there are ledges and eaves on Tower's facade that might give someone a foothold on the way down." Mrs. Cook poked her head out the window for a moment. "The person probably slipped inside a window on one of the lower floors," she said, drawing her head back inside before shutting the window. "I'll have to make an announcement of this at dinner—maybe someone noticed a person climbing down."

"Was anything out of place in your office?" Nancy asked.

"The elevator door was wide open, of course—with the cables exposed. An open door like that would have automatically stopped a moving elevator." She marched over to the elevator door and pointed to something on the floor nearby. "Take a look at this, Nancy. It's a saw for cutting metal."

Nancy studied the saw without touching it. She didn't want to disturb the evidence in case Mrs. Cook called in the police. The saw was a nasty-looking instrument with small, sharp teeth that resembled an evil grin.

"Did you notice how badly the cable was damaged?" Nancy asked.

"There were nicks where the person had cut into it," Mrs. Cook explained, "but I don't think he or she had enough time to cause any damage. Of course, I'll have to get the elevator mechanics to check it, but I think you were very lucky, Nancy—another ten minutes, and you might have been sent plunging to the sub-basement." Mrs. Cook shot Nancy a puzzled look. "But what were you doing in the elevator, anyway?"

"You asked to see me. I was just responding to your note."

"What note, dear?" Mrs. Cook asked. "I never sent you a note."

Nancy pulled Mrs. Cook's message out of her pants pocket and handed it to her. "This—you put it in my mail slot in Mr. Moralis's office."

"I never wrote this," the headmistress said, peering at it. She adjusted her reading glasses, which hung around her neck on a cord, and added indignantly, "You were duped, Nancy. This note is a forgery. The Black Cat must have stolen my stationery and typed this message to lure you into the elevator, knowing that I wouldn't be in my office."

Nancy cast her mind back over the past hour, remembering that Mr. Moralis had left his office for a short errand before he'd found the note in her mail cubby. Someone must have delivered it while he was gone, she realized.

"I'm definitely going to lock my elevator door after this!" Mrs. Cook declared as she walked wearily back to her desk and sat down behind it. She pressed her fingers together to form a steeple and gazed over them at Nancy. "I think it's time for me to call in the police. You were in serious danger, Nancy, and we don't know that other girls won't be in danger, too. What if one of our students gets hurt? Waverly's reputation is already on shaky ground, with many parents calling up, frantic about the curse notes. If something really bad did happen to a student, I'm afraid the school would have to close."

"I think you should wait to call the police," Nancy said calmly. "I understand why you're worried, but there's a better chance of catching the person off guard if the police aren't around. If the next prank is also dangerous, I agree that you'll have to alert them. The girls' safety is more important than anything."

"Yes, it is," Mrs. Cook said. "It's even more important than catching this dreadful person. Don't forget, Nancy—the mere presence of the police might scare the Cat off, and then our problem would be solved."

"But when the police leave, the Cat might strike again," Nancy pointed out. "I think we can hold off on calling them for just a little while longer."

"Well . . . I'll leave the investigation to you for now, Nancy," Mrs. Cook said.

Nancy took a moment to gather her thoughts. So far, she hadn't zeroed in on any suspects, though she remembered Eliza McBride's strange accusations about Francesca. But even if Francesca was the only person who could touch Tassie, why would she have wanted to put the cat inside her teacher's drawer?

"Mrs. Cook," Nancy said, "can you think of anyone who holds a grudge against Waverly? I'm thinking that the Black Cat's goal might be to close down the school. If people get scared enough by the curses, you said yourself that Waverly might have to shut down."

"Hmm. Someone who holds a grudge," Mrs. Cook said thoughtfully, tucking a lock of her gray hair behind her ear. "Well, the first person who pops into my mind is Eliza McBride. I've suspected her from the beginning, but I didn't want my opinion to influence you."

"Eliza?" Nancy said, surprised. "But she was a victim herself."

"Maybe Eliza staged her own curse so that no one would suspect her," Mrs. Cook guessed.

"Maybe," Nancy said. She told Mrs. Cook about Eliza accusing Francesca of masterminding the curses in Ms. Friedlander's class.

"That girl!" Mrs. Cook said, hitting her desk with her fist in outrage. "She's out of line. But Eliza's outburst is a perfect example of why I suspect her. She's always been a mischief maker, with spirits that are too high for her own good."

"But has she done anything in particular that makes you suspect her?" Nancy asked. "I mean, lots of girls have high spirits and are mischievous at times."

"Whenever I've had a talk with Eliza about her behavior, she'll tell me how much she hates Waverly," Mrs. Cook said. "She even claimed she'd be happy if it shut down so her parents couldn't force her to attend."

"But if she wants to leave, couldn't she just get herself kicked out?" Nancy asked. "That would be easier than shutting down the whole school."

"I can see Eliza wanting to bring the school down with her," Mrs. Cook said. "She's the dramatic type and likes to create a stir. By the way, Nancy, I hope you'll attend the opening of *Camelot* this evening. You can get another good look at Eliza."

"I'd love to see the play," Nancy said, smiling. "And I'll watch Eliza closely. But I'd also like to know a little more about Francesca."

"Francesca Marco is an exchange student from Italy, and a junior," Mrs. Cook explained. "It's true that Catastrophe lets Francesca hold him—I've seen her pick him up and even get him to purr. He hisses at everyone else. She's the only person I can think of who'd be able to put that animal in a desk drawer, so I can see why she'd get linked to the Black Cat curses. Still . . . there's never been any hint that she bears the school ill will."

The shadows in Mrs. Cook's office reminded Nancy of the time. Five-thirty, she saw, checking her watch. Outside, the sky was darkening into a violet-colored dusk.

"We've got to get ready for dinner now, Nancy," Mrs. Cook announced, switching on a lamp. "It starts promptly in the dining hall at six."

"Okay," Nancy said. "I'll keep an eye on both Eliza and Francesca—and report back to you. There's just one more thing I want to mention." Nancy filled Mrs. Cook in about the black cat illustration in *Famous American Short Stories* and then asked if she could search Eliza's and Francesca's rooms for a copy of the book or a stamp.

"By all means, Nancy," Mrs. Cook replied. "Eliza's room is in Blackbird, the senior dorm, and Francesca lives in Sparrow with the other juniors. Just be careful that no one sees you sneaking around."

Nancy asked Mrs. Cook if she could find out whether the book was ever assigned reading for a class and if the library stocked it. After scrolling through a couple of files in her computer, Mrs. Cook said, "No to both your questions, Nancy. There's no reason for this book to be floating around the school, so if a student has it, I'd say that's a gigantic clue, especially because we know that the Black Cat couldn't have borrowed it from the library to make the stamp."

Nancy thanked her. As she was leaving through the stairway door, Mrs. Cook flashed her a grateful smile and added, "I'm so glad you and George are here to help."

"Lucky us—third-row seats," Bess murmured. Her parents had just dropped her off at the Waverly auditorium, where Nancy and George were waiting with *Camelot* tickets.

After Nancy's talk with Mrs. Cook, she'd called Bess to invite her to the performance that evening. Maybe Bess and George will have some interesting thoughts about Eliza, Nancy hoped.

As the three girls took seats among the faculty, students, and parents of cast members, a tall girl with long auburn hair on Nancy's left turned toward her. Nancy recoiled in surprise. The girl was wearing a pair of pointy fifties-type eyeglasses with plastic black cats in the corners. But before Nancy could comment, the curtain rose.

A girl dressed as King Arthur strode forward followed by another one dressed as Merlin. After King Arthur sang an introductory song about the kingdom of Camelot, Eliza swept onstage, wearing a long blond wig. Flinging out her arms, she turned toward the audience and opened her mouth to sing.

Eliza's gaze suddenly focused on the third row. Her body stiffened. Then she pointed at the girl with the glasses and screamed, filling the theater to the rafters with her terrified sound.

Before Nancy could figure out what was happening, Eliza crumpled to the floor in a dead faint.

7

A Sticky Investigation

The girl with the glasses jolted upright in her seat, gaping at Eliza's motionless form. The audience gasped. For a split second there was total silence, and then everyone started speaking at once.

A young man rushed out on stage and gestured for the audience to be quiet. "Is there a doctor in the house?" he yelled.

Even before he finished speaking, a tall curly-haired woman rushed up from the audience. "I'm Dr. Slingluff," she announced, "Lucy's mother. Let me take a look at Eliza." Bending down, Dr. Slingluff felt Eliza's pulse. After a moment Dr. Slingluff drew a small vial out of her purse and placed it under Eliza's nose.

Eliza sat up abruptly, shaking her head. Her wig slid

forward over her eyes. As she pushed it back, her eyes focused on the man who had called for a doctor. "Mr. Frederick," she said, looking wildly about her. "What's that gross-smelling stuff?"

"Smelling salts," he told her. "You just fainted."

"Eliza, I'd like you to rest backstage for a moment," Dr. Slingluff said.

Facing the audience, Mr. Frederick announced, "For those of you who don't know me, I'm John Frederick, the drama teacher at Waverly. We'll take a ten-minute break now, but please stay in your seats—*Camelot* will go on as planned, with either Eliza or her understudy."

Supported by Mr. Frederick, Eliza hobbled backstage, followed by King Arthur and Merlin, while Dr. Slingluff returned to her seat. Nancy turned to Bess and George. "I'm going to try to ask Eliza a few questions."

Backstage, Nancy found Eliza slumped in a chair, with her long blue medieval-style dress swirling around her legs and her wig in a heap on the floor beside her. Nancy was relieved to see that Mr. Frederick was on the other side of the room, talking to a girl dressed as a knight.

"How are you feeling, Eliza?" Nancy asked.

Eliza raised her face to Nancy's. At her pale and stricken look, Nancy instantly stopped suspecting Eliza of faking her fainting spell to get attention.

"Better," Eliza answered feebly. "Who are you?"

"Don't you remember me from Ms. Friedlander's class?" Nancy asked. "I'm Nancy Drew, her teaching intern. I was hoping you'd feel up to answering a few questions."

"Sure. Whatever," Eliza mumbled.

"I wondered why the girl wearing the cat glasses disturbed you so much," Nancy said.

Eliza shot up in her chair. "Disturbed me! That's putting it mildly, Ms. Drew. Lila could have *killed* me!"

"But why?" Nancy asked, surprised by Eliza's strong reaction. "What's so shocking about a pair of glasses with black cats on them? The girl—Lila—was probably trying to make a stir by spoofing the curses with her glasses. She acted out of line and everything, but still—"

"Out of line!" Eliza mimicked in a rude, sarcastic tone. "Give me a break, Ms. Drew. Lila was guilty of a *premeditated* attack on me—and me alone. She knew I'd gotten a curse note, and she meant to upset me by wearing those weird black cat glasses. She wanted to rub it in that I've been cursed."

"But why would she want to get at you?" Nancy asked.

"Jealousy," Eliza wailed. "Lila's jealous of me because she wanted to play Guinevere. She tried out for the part, and Mr. Frederick narrowed down his choices to either her or me. Obviously, she's burning up with envy."

"That's ridiculous, Eliza, and you know it!" came a girl's voice to Nancy's right. Nancy wheeled around. Standing by a backstage door was Lila—but this time without her glasses.

Eliza's wide green eyes narrowed into angry slits as she focused on Lila. "What are you doing back here?" she asked fiercely. "You have a lot of nerve." Craning her neck as she glanced around the room, she called for Mr. Frederick, but he was nowhere in sight.

"I came backstage to tell you how sorry I am for upsetting you, Eliza," Lila said. "You know how nearsighted I am, and my regular glasses were mysteriously swapped for these cat ones. These aren't my prescription, but they're better than nothing. I had to wear them tonight just so I could see the play."

"A likely story, Lila Van Voorhies!" Eliza protested. "I'm surprised you can look yourself in the mirror with all your lies."

"I came back here to apologize," Lila repeated. "I had no idea you'd be so upset by these glasses or I would never have worn them."

Eliza stared sullenly at Lila, biting her lip. Meanwhile, Lila opened up her purse and rummaged around inside. "I can't believe someone stole my glasses," she murmured, "I keep hoping I've just misplaced them."

Her hand froze inside her purse.

"What's wrong?" Nancy asked.

Lila drew out a legal-size envelope with her first name printed on it. She opened it with trembling hands.

The envelope fell to the floor as Lila unfolded the message inside. Sure enough, it was a curse note, Nancy saw—identical to the others.

"I'd better show this note to Mrs. Cook," Lila said. "I noticed her sitting in an aisle seat in the fifth or sixth row."

Nancy and Lila told Eliza they hoped she'd feel better soon and then left in search of Mrs. Cook. Lila mentioned to Nancy that she'd discovered the cat glasses on her desk when she returned from taking a shower before the play.

"Someone must have come into my room while I was showering, swapped the glasses, and then put this note in my purse," she explained to Nancy. Shivering, she added, "I realize other people have gotten notes too, but when it happens to you, it's *really* creepy."

After showing Mrs. Cook the note, Nancy and Lila returned to their seats. A minute later the auditorium lights dimmed, the stage lights came on, and Eliza paraded confidently on to the stage as if nothing had happened.

"I can't see much," Lila whispered to Nancy, "but I don't dare put on those glasses again. She'll go bananas and faint."

"I wouldn't," Nancy agreed, and grinned. "After all, we don't want to be here all night."

During Act II, Nancy leaned toward George and Bess and whispered, "I don't think I'm learning anything new about this case by watching Eliza. I might as well use this time to search her room."

"Good thinking," Bess whispered back. "And since

Eliza's stuck onstage, you won't have to worry about her barging in on you. But you'd better hurry. I've seen this play before, and we're almost at the end."

Nancy excused herself as she left the theater, then hurried toward Blackbird, the seniors' dorm. Following a path past Shakespeare, where Ms. Friedlander taught her classes, Nancy jogged up to a yellow clapboard house with green shutters and a sign saying "Blackbird" over the front door.

Nancy hadn't seen one person on her way from the theater to the dorm. I might as well be on another planet, she thought, shivering against the cold night wind. A full moon had lit her way to Blackbird, but as she stood at the dormitory door, clouds scudded over the moon and a creepy darkness fell over the school grounds.

Nancy heard a high-pitched squeal. Tassie? she thought, startled. But after a moment she decided it was just the squeak of a car wheel on a road nearby.

Nancy pushed open the door of Blackbird, grateful to be entering a cheerfully lit house, even if no one else was there. She quickly shut the door behind her and got to work scanning the name plaques of the rooms.

On the second floor Nancy found a room labeled McBride/Chang. This must belong to Eliza and her roommate, Nancy reasoned.

She slipped inside and shut the door. What a mess, she thought as she crept around shoes, clothes, books, papers, and pens, which made an obstacle course on the floor.

Nancy searched the bookshelf for *Famous American Short Stories*. No luck. Then she headed toward one of the two closets.

Good, this one's hers, she thought, noting Eliza's name written in permanent marker on the inside collar of a coat. Now, let me see what's here.

Pushing aside some shirts and skirts, Nancy scanned the closet floor. There was a bucket in the corner behind some dresses. Strange, she thought. A bucket in a girl's closet?

Nancy pulled out the bucket and pried off the lid. The bucket was full of a black sticky substance. She sniffed it, wrinkling her nose at the acrid smell. Tar!

Tar had been used on Lucy Slingluff's sneakers before her basketball game, Nancy remembered.

Footsteps pounded down the hall. Nancy froze as the door handle rattled. Someone was about to come in!

8

The Nightmare Note

Eliza's door burst open. Nancy's heart raced. She couldn't shut the closet door without risking being seen.

In a flash Nancy slid the bucket of tar into the corner. Then she shrank back among Eliza's clothes, pulling them around her and hoping for the best.

She held her breath as soft footsteps entered the room.

"Nancy, if you're hiding somewhere, please come out—it's only me!" she heard Bess call.

Flinging Eliza's clothes aside, Nancy rushed out of the closet. "I thought you might be Eliza," she said, grinning at Bess with relief.

"Well, she'll probably be back pretty soon," Bess said, "after she's bored with everyone congratulating her. Anyway, the play's over, and other students will be back, too, so let's get out of here."

"How'd you know where Eliza's room was?" Nancy asked, smiling.

"George introduced me to Mrs. Cook as the audience was filing out and she told me," Bess said. "By the way, George is waiting for us by your car—let's go!"

Nancy and Bess slipped through the front door of Blackbird just as a group of girls turned the corner of the path leading to their dorm. "No one saw us—don't worry," Nancy assured Bess. "We were just in time."

Back at the faculty parking lot behind Tower, Nancy and Bess found George leaning against Nancy's Mustang. "Did you find any clues?" George asked curiously.

"You bet," Nancy said, unlocking her car. Once everyone was inside, Nancy started the engine and told her friends about the bucket of tar.

"Whoa!" George said. "Well, if you ask me, Eliza's the one."

"Wait till you hear what I discovered during intermission," Bess said proudly.

"What?" Nancy and George asked in unison.

"I eavesdropped on some girls in front of me in the soda line," Bess said. "They mentioned that for the past few months, Eliza had wanted short hair, and she was annoyed that Mr. Frederick was making her wait until after the play to cut it. He'd insisted that her character have long hair. Sorry I couldn't tell you all this earlier,

64

guys, but I'd barely gotten my soda when the music for Act Two started."

"Hmm," George murmured, "so maybe Eliza's curse was really a blessing in disguise."

"But in that case, why would she send so many other people curses?" Bess asked. "She could accomplish her goal by just sending one to herself."

"Because her goal wasn't just to cut her hair," Nancy said. "It's to close down the school. She's just making herself seem less suspicious if she gets a curse, too."

"Eliza looks pretty guilty," Bess declared. Nancy frowned. "Still, how was she able to get Tassie into Ms. Friedlander's drawer? From what we've heard, Francesca's the only one who can handle him. I'm going to search Francesca's room first thing tomorrow, the minute she goes to class."

The next morning Nancy pulled her Mustang into the faculty parking lot at Waverly just as breakfast was ending.

As she and George climbed out of the car and locked it, Nancy pulled her scarf tight against the cold winter wind. "The weather really has changed since yesterday," she mused.

"That's for sure," George said, shivering. She glanced up at the lead-colored sky. "I can almost imagine snow in the forecast."

"Hmm, maybe we'll get stuck here at school with the

Black Cat," Nancy said dryly. "By the way, George, any chance you could be a lookout while I search Francesca's room? I don't have a class first period."

"Sorry, Nan," George said as the girls headed down the main walk toward Tower to check their mail. "Ms. Kahn wants me to help coach ninth-grade basketball in the gym this morning. I'll see you later."

Just then a girl dashed across the lawn toward Tower. Her dark eyes were brimming with tears, and her expression was terrified. Nancy stopped, full of foreboding.

"It's been stolen!" the girl screamed. "I've been cursed!"

"Wait, stop!" Nancy commanded as the girl pounded past her. "Let me help you."

The girl spun around. "A whole semester's work—down the drain!" she wailed.

Nancy placed a calming hand on the girl's arm. "Tell us what happened," she said evenly.

Clutching frantically at her short black hair, the girl said, "My senior thesis was deleted from my computer, and the backup disk was taken. It's due tomorrow, before we leave for our long winter weekend. I've been working on it since October."

"You say you got a curse note?" Nancy asked.

"Yes—left on my computer while I was eating breakfast," the girl said, waving the envelope around.

"Let's go tell Mrs. Cook," Nancy suggested. "She'll want to know right away."

Nancy, George, and the girl, who introduced herself as Kaleesha Jones, hurried into Tower to tell Mr. Moralis that they needed to see Mrs. Cook immediately. Three minutes later they stepped off the elevator into her office.

"This is shameful!" Mrs. Cook said, staring in shock at Kaleesha's curse note. "How dare this person steal your work?" To Nancy and George, the headmistress said, "Kaleesha is a straight-A senior, number one in the class. Ms. Friedlander tells me she's been working hard on her paper all year. Next to your elevator mishap, Nancy, this is a serious offense."

"What'll I do?" Kaleesha asked. "Will Ms. Friedlander flunk me?"

"No, dear, this isn't your fault," Mrs. Cook said firmly. "Don't worry—we'll figure something out."

Kaleesha's lip quivered. "Thank you, Mrs. Cook. But nothing can bring back my work!"

"I understand your distress," Mrs. Cook said sympathetically. "All I can say is that we'll try our hardest to find this person and get your work back. Let's have faith that we'll succeed. In the meantime, you need to run along. You're late for class—history, is it?"

Kaleesha nodded and thanked Mrs. Cook. After she'd left, Nancy told Mrs. Cook about the tar in Eliza's closet. "Lucy Slingluff's sneakers were covered with tar," Nancy said, "so this is real evidence against Eliza."

"I'd say so!" Mrs. Cook exclaimed, horrified. "There's no *other* reason I can think of for a student to keep a bucket of tar in her closet. I think you've found our Black Cat, Nancy."

"Not necessarily," Nancy said. "I'd like to gather more evidence against Eliza first. If we grilled her about the tar now, without other evidence, she could offer some innocent reason for having it."

"I've got another reason for suspecting Eliza," Mrs. Cook went on. "You see, she and Lila Van Voorhies are rivals for control of the 'cool' group of seniors—with Lila edging Eliza out in popularity. Even though they're part of the same clique, they're not friends. If anyone has it in for Lila, Eliza would be the one."

"Which would explain why Lila got her curse note," George remarked.

"That's right," Mrs. Cook said.

After saying goodbye to Mrs. Cook and heading outside, the two girls went their separate ways. George headed for the gym, while Nancy followed a path toward Sparrow, a Cape Cod–style shingle cottage separated from Blackbird by an ivy-covered stone wall.

Nancy slipped into Francesca's dorm, which was so quiet it seemed as if it were holding its breath. She found Francesca's single room on the third floor.

Nancy checked her watch. One more minute till the bell would ring. Adrenaline shot through her. There's no way I'll be on time for Ms. Freidlander's class, she realized, and even worse, Francesca might have a free period next and discover me snooping.

Nancy scanned the hastily made bed, the laundry scattered over the rug, and the bureau and desk piled high with books and papers. This room is even messier than Eliza's, she thought—I'll just focus on the bookshelf.

The neatly stacked shelves of books between the two windows suggested that Francesca rarely bothered with them.

Nancy pored through the books. Just as the bell echoed through Sparrow, her eyes lit on a battered red book, exactly the same color as Bess's. She squinted at the book's spine, but the old print was impossible to read. With growing excitement, Nancy yanked the book out of the shelf and opened it to the cover page.

A thrill went through her as she read *Famous American Short Stories* on the worn page. Flipping to "The Black Cat," Nancy saw the same image that appeared on the curse notes, minus the red eyes and vampire teeth.

Nancy's pulse raced. The top corner of the page was turned down, as if the owner had marked it.

Nancy slapped the book shut triumphantly. I bet Francesca knows a lot more about the Black Cat curses than she's letting on, Nancy thought.

She stuck the book back into the shelf, so Francesca wouldn't be alerted that someone suspected her. Then she dashed back downstairs and hurried down the path toward Shakespeare. As she jogged along, the second bell rang out from a nearby building.

I'm late, Nancy thought, gritting her teeth. I hope Ms. Friedlander won't get mad—she seems kind of strict.

When Nancy arrived in the classroom, Ms. Friedlander wasn't there.

"Where could she be, Ms. Drew?" a curly-haired girl moaned. "She's never late."

"Did she tell you she'd be held up?" a ponytailed girl asked impatiently. "I mean, we've been waiting five whole minutes, and she's supposed to give us an exam today."

"I haven't seen Ms. Friedlander today," Nancy replied, "but I'm sure she has a good explanation for why she's not here. Let's wait a couple more minutes. If she still hasn't come, I'll call Mrs. Cook from the hall phone."

Despite her reassuring words, Nancy felt a twinge of worry. If Ms. Friedlander was never late, then where was she? Was there a real possibility that something bad had happened to her?

Five minutes later Nancy was on the phone with the headmistress. "I haven't seen her since breakfast," Mrs. Cook told Nancy. "But she had first period free. I assume she's working in her apartment and lost track of the time."

"I'm concerned about her because of all the curses," Nancy said.

"You're right to worry, Nancy," Mrs. Cook declared. "Will you meet me at Blue Jay in ten minutes? It's the faculty apartment house on the other side of Sparrow. Tell your class to work ahead on their English assignments."

"Okay," Nancy said, and hung up. Ten minutes later she and Mrs. Cook were knocking on Ms. Friedlander's apartment door.

"There's no answer," Nancy said tensely.

Mrs. Cook knocked louder. Still, no response.

"I've got a master key to all the apartments," Mrs. Cook explained, taking a large ring of keys out of her purse.

Seconds later she turned the lock with her key, and she and Nancy entered a small living room. "Oh, no!" Mrs. Cook exclaimed, aghast.

Nancy gaped at the overturned chairs and tables and the books and papers scattered everywhere. "It looks as if there's been a struggle," she said.

She walked over to a closed door. "That's the bedroom," Mrs. Cook told her.

Nancy's stomach churned as she opened the door and glanced inside.

The room was empty. Nancy gestured for Mrs. Cook to follow her. Unlike the living room, the bedroom was orderly. The only unusual object was a white envelope on the bed. Unlike the curse notes, it had no name on the outside.

Quickly Nancy opened the envelope. Inside was a typed note to Mr. and Mrs. Friedlander—Ms. Friedlander's parents, Nancy assumed.

Nancy started reading the note to Mrs. Cook. " 'Five million big ones by tomorrow at 5:00 P.M.," it began, "or you'll never see your darling daughter again.' "

9

One More Suspect

"Oh, no!" Mrs. Cook breathed, her face ashen. She slumped into a nearby chair, dropping her face in her hands.

"There's more," Nancy said, glancing over the note. "The kidnapper wants Mr. and Mrs. Friedlander to place the money in a waterproof envelope and deliver it to a cat-shaped urn at Hilltop Cemetery. The note's signed 'The Black Cat.'" Nancy looked over at Mrs. Cook.

Mrs. Cook raised her head. "As you probably know, Hilltop Cemetery is a short walk from school, not far from a boys' school called Granger Academy, where Waverly girls often go for proms. But the terrible thing is—Angela Friedlander's parents are dead! And I'm sure she isn't rich herself. How are we going to raise the ransom money by tomorrow afternoon?"

"I don't know," Nancy said, frowning. "Raising that kind of money sounds impossible. There's only one solution that I can see—we'll have to catch the Black Cat before then."

"Oh, Nancy, do you really think that's possible?" Mrs. Cook asked hopefully.

"Yes," Nancy said firmly, trying to sound more convinced than she felt. "But it's definitely time to call the police. I'll keep going with my investigation while they conduct theirs."

"I'll call them from here," Mrs. Cook said, picking up the phone beside Ms. Friedlander's bed. Before dialing, she added, "I'm worried that other curse victims are in danger of getting kidnapped."

"I'm worried about that, too," Nancy confessed. "I think you should warn those girls to be on guard. Also, the police should know who they are so they can keep a watch on them."

Nancy told Mrs. Cook about finding *Famous American Short Stories* in Francesca's bookshelf with the dog eared page.

"We should question that girl right away," Mrs. Cook said.

"I'll question her later," Nancy said. "There's a chance the book was planted on her shelf—just as there's a chance someone framed Eliza with the tar."

After Mrs. Cook called the police, she and Nancy left to meet them. Outside Blue Jay, Mrs. Cook pointed out Ms. Friedlander's car, which was in a small cul-de-sac on the far side of the building.

Noticing that the car doors were unlocked, Nancy slid inside. She couldn't find any obvious clues, but as she checked behind the visor over the driver's seat, a set of car keys dropped out. Nancy put them back, and she and Mrs. Cook hurried on to Tower. In the time before the police showed up, the head-mistress interrupted classes to call an emergency assembly to inform students and faculty of the kid-napping.

The moment the students learned that Ms. Fried-lander had been kidnapped, the atmosphere of the school completely changed. There were no more groups of excited girls chatting in the common room; no rock music wafted out of dormitory windows. There were no sounds of laughter anywhere. Everyone—students and faculty—seemed frightened and shocked.

When the police came, Mrs. Cook and Nancy filled them in on the details of the curses and Ms. Friedlander's disappearance. As they all stood on the front steps of Tower, Chief McGinnis announced, "We'll dust Ms. Friedlander's apartment for fingerprints right now. It's good that you two didn't touch the overturned furniture. We'll also talk privately to the girls who received notes. Any little detail they can provide might be helpful. And I'd like to warn them to be on guard. I'll alert my officers to keep a special watch on them."

"We'll be searching the school buildings," his associate, Detective Ghent, said, "and we'll station officers on campus around the clock. I'll stay here myself until my shift ends at midnight."

"Waverly Academy is closing for a four-day midwinter break tomorrow at noon," Mrs. Cook told them. "We resume classes on Tuesday morning." She sighed. "At least the girls will get a rest from all this."

"We'll try to have this mystery solved before everyone goes away," Chief McGinniss said. "If we don't, you might have to postpone Tuesday's opening just to ensure the girls' safety."

Nancy thought about telling the police her suspicions of Eliza and Francesca. She reasoned that Ms. Friedlander might be found more quickly if the police were constantly trailing those girls.

She quickly rejected that idea, though. First, the police were pretty noticeable, and if either girl realized she was being followed, the guilty one would just lie low and stay away from Ms. Friedlander. Maybe she'd even stop bringing her food.

Also, Nancy thought the police might doubt that Eliza or Francesca would have the strength to kidnap Ms. Friedlander and take her to a hiding place. But she reasoned that either girl could have sneaked up on Ms. Friedlander and knocked her unconscious with a weapon. Since both girls were old enough to drive, either one of them could have transported her in Ms. Friedlander's own car. After all, the keys were inside it, and it was parked on the far side of Blue Jay—not visible to the rest of the school.

Mr. Moralis hurried outside, handing a stack of telephone messages to Mrs. Cook. "All these parents have called up, sounding frantic," he told her. "They want to pull their daughters out of school this minute—and they want to keep them out until the Black Cat is caught."

Before Mrs. Cook could respond, Mr. Frederick approached her. "Are you sure it's safe for us to be at school?" he asked anxiously. "I'm trying to teach a drama class now, and everyone's too scared to concentrate."

"Maybe I *should* close the school," Mrs. Cook said. "Everyone's panicking—and with good reason. People are in danger."

Nancy placed a calming hand on Mrs. Cook's arm and took her aside. "I think we've got a better chance of catching the Black Cat under cover of the regular school routine," she whispered. "After all, my two suspects are students. If they went on vacation now, they'd probably just pretend to go away and then hide out till they got the ransom money. We wouldn't be able to find them."

"As usual, Nancy, you give good advice," Mrs. Cook declared as the bell for the next class rang. "And I'm confident that with your help we'll catch this person."

During the next period, Nancy proctored another

class of Ms. Friedlander's. While the girls worked on an essay, Nancy took a moment to think about her case. What did all the people who got curse notes have in common? she wondered. Why was the Black Cat targeting them? As far as Nancy knew, all they had in common was Waverly Academy. Nancy decided to talk to each of them after class. Maybe there would be something in their backgrounds to link them to one of her suspects.

The bell rang, and Nancy and the students went to lunch. In the dining hall Nancy found George and updated her about the book in Francesca's room. She also mentioned that she needed help questioning the girls who had received curse notes.

"Now is a perfect time to round them up, because it's lunch period—free time," Nancy said. "Why don't I talk to Lucy, Sindu, and Eliza, and you take Lila and Kaleesha? We can talk to them casually without breaking our cover, but any detail we learn about them might be important."

"Obviously we can't talk to Ms. Friedlander," George remarked, "but maybe I'll ask Mrs. Cook where she was from and stuff."

"Good thinking, George," Nancy said. "I'll meet you on the steps of Tower in half an hour."

George gave Nancy a thumbs-up sign, then headed off to Blackbird to find Lila and Kaleesha, while Nancy went upstairs to track down Sindu.

Twenty minutes later Nancy had finished talking to both Lucy and Sindu and was now hurrying toward Blackbird to round up Eliza. Nancy sighed as she climbed the front steps of the dorm. Nothing in Lucy's and Sindu's backgrounds had offered the slightest clue.

Upstairs, Nancy poked her head into Eliza's room, but it was empty. She chewed her lip, feeling frustrated. Where was Eliza? She hadn't been in the common room when Nancy had checked it a few minutes ago. And when Nancy had telephoned the theater, Mr. Frederick had told her that she wasn't there, either.

Nancy felt a growing suspicion. If Eliza wasn't around school, could that mean she was with Ms. Friedlander in a secret hiding place? Eliza had better have a good explanation for where she's been, Nancy thought.

On her way back to Tower to meet George, Nancy ran into Francesca.

"Hey!" Nancy said as Francesca trudged along with her eyes to the ground, oblivious of her surroundings. "Do you have a moment?"

Francesca started in alarm. She gazed at Nancy blankly, as if she'd never laid eyes on her before. "Why . . . what do you want?" she asked tentatively.

"Don't you remember me? I'm Ms. Friedlander's intern," Nancy said.

"Oh, yes," Francesca mumbled. "I remember."

"I understand you're an exchange student from Italy," Nancy said.

"From Milan," Francesca said in a soft dreamy voice.

"Did you know any of the girls at Waverly before you came here?" Nancy asked.

"I knew nothing about this school before I came here—except that it had a class called Animals in Literature." Francesca's eyes glowed. "I came here because I wanted to learn about cute animals."

"You mean the class you refuse to do homework for?" Nancy asked.

Francesca raised her brows. "I *would* do the work, if only I liked Ms. Friedlander better."

"You don't like her?" Nancy asked. "Why not?"

"Well . . . she's kind of strict," Francesca said. "I don't see why I should do any work for someone so strict."

"She may be a little strict," Nancy commented, "but she's not that bad. I mean, she didn't make you go to Detention when you hadn't done your homework all year long."

Francesca pursed her lips, as if she couldn't quite follow Nancy's train of thought.

"Have you heard of an old book called *Famous American Short Stories?*" Nancy asked, changing the subject.

"I don't think so," Francesca said. "Why?"

"Because I saw a copy of it in Ms. Friedlander's desk," Nancy fudged. "I wondered if she'd assigned it to any of her classes—like maybe the Animals in Literature class, for instance."

"No," Francesca said. "Not to that class. Maybe she

assigned it to one of her senior English classes—I wouldn't know."

"So you've never heard of it?"

"No," Francesca said nonchalantly. "But why do you care so much about this book?"

"Because it has a drawing of a black cat that looks exactly like the one on the curse notes," Nancy replied.

"Really?" Francesca asked, her brown eyes wide. "Wow! So . . . uh, what does that mean?"

Nancy resisted the urge to smile at Francesca's spacey manner. Was she for real? Nancy wondered. Or was she just putting on an act to make herself seem innocent?

"I understand you feed Catastrophe, the big black cat who hangs out at school," Nancy went on, ignoring Francesca's question.

"I can't resist him," Francesca said with a goofy grin.

"Obviously, he trusts you. Are you sure you didn't put him in Ms. Friedlander's desk drawer? Not meaning to scare her, of course, and not that you wrote her the curse note," Nancy added quickly, "but just to give Tassie a comfortable place to sleep."

"Comfortable!" Francesca exclaimed hotly. "That drawer must have been cramped and scary for that poor cat. I'd never put Tassie anywhere near Ms. Friedlander—she's too mean." Flashing Nancy an uncertain smile, she added, "And now I have to go. It's free time, and I don't want to waste another minute of it talking."

Nancy watched as Francesca hurried down the path. What's she in such a rush for? she wondered. Nancy was tempted to follow her but saw that it was time to meet George.

Back on the front stairs of Tower, Nancy learned that George had discovered from Mr. Moralis that Ms. Friedlander was from Portland, Oregon, and this was her first year at Waverly. She'd moved to River Heights in the fall.

"I couldn't find Lila anywhere," George explained, "but I talked to Kaleesha. She said she's from Minneapolis, and Lila's from Los Angeles. I couldn't figure out any link between them and the Black Cat."

Nancy told George her part of the story.

"We've hit a brick wall!" George moaned. "Though Francesca was acting kind of suspicious if you ask me. Do you think she could have been rushing off to check on Ms. Friedlander?"

"Maybe," Nancy said. "Or maybe that's why Eliza's missing."

"Eliza's in the art studio," a familiar voice said at her elbow. Nancy whirled around and saw Kaleesha Jones dressed in a Waverly sports tunic and a winter parka. "I was on my way to gym class when I heard you say that Eliza was missing," Kaleesha explained. "Trust me, she's alive and well. I was working in Picasso— the art building—when she came in ten minutes ago."

"Thanks," Nancy said. As Kaleesha left them, the bell announcing afternoon classes rang out from

Tower. "I'd better hurry over there," Nancy told George.

"And I have to get to the gym," George said. "See you later, Nan."

Nancy jogged toward Picasso, a large modern building with huge glass windows and skylights. Inside, Nancy found Eliza washing paint brushes. She wore a spattered smock over her gym tunic.

"Can I talk to you for a moment?" Nancy asked.

"Better be quick," Eliza said, "or I'll be late for gym."

"Uh, the police found a bucket of tar in your closet," Nancy fudged, unwilling to admit that she was an undercover detective and had been snooping in her room. "They're busy, so I told them I'd ask you about it. They were curious to know what you were doing with tar, because of Lucy Slingluff's sneakers."

Eliza drew herself up, her eyes flashing outrage. "Are they accusing me of being the Black Cat? I'm going to sue them for slander! I don't know anything about a bucket of tar in my closet. The police probably planted it there." Eliza threw her brushes in the sink, yanked off her smock, then grabbed her coat from a hook by the door. "Goodbye and good riddance! I'm late." She slammed the door behind her in a huff.

Nancy let a few seconds go by before following Eliza out the door. Is she really on her way to the gym? Nancy wondered as she trailed Eliza from a distance of twenty yards. A few minutes later the athletic complex loomed beyond a curve in the path.

Nancy watched carefully as Eliza went inside. A few minutes later Nancy slipped into the gym after her.

Inside, two teams of girls were furiously playing basketball, while George and Ms. Kahn were following them on the sidelines with whistles in their mouths.

"Hey, Eliza, pass it to me!" a tall, chestnut-haired girl yelled.

Eliza tossed the basketball to the girl. But just as the girl was about to catch it, a heavyset girl with short black hair intercepted the pass. Nancy recognized the black-haired girl—Ms. Friedlander had spoken sternly to her after her senior English class, Nancy remembered.

The instant she caught the ball, the black-haired girl leaped up and neatly threw it through her hoop. Then she pumped her arms triumphantly into the air—knocking into Eliza in her zeal.

"Ow!" Eliza exclaimed, falling backward onto the floor. "You idiot!" She clambered to her feet, her face red with fury. Pointing at the girl, Eliza screamed, "I demand an apology. And no way should that basket count!"

"Rosie knocked you down after she took the shot, Eliza," Ms. Kahn pointed out. "But I'm sure she'd be happy to apologize to you."

Rosie crossed her arms belligerently. "I will not!

Eliza's faking. She fell down on purpose—just so my basket wouldn't count."

"You . . . liar!" Eliza sputtered. She glared speechlessly at Rosie for a moment, before finding her tongue. "You kidnapped Ms. Friedlander, Tsing!" she yelled. "Admit it—she accused you of cheating, and you want revenge!"

10

Eliza's Accusation

Eliza's words echoed through the gym. For a moment everyone was silent. Then Ms. Kahn fixed her ice blue eyes on Eliza, as if she were an opponent in a duel.

"I want you to march right over to Detention, Eliza," Ms. Kahn said tersely. "There's no excuse for those hateful words."

As Eliza stormed away, Nancy took George aside and told her that Eliza had denied knowing about the bucket of tar.

"She can deny it till she's blue in the face," George said in a disgusted tone. "I still think she's guilty. I mean, she's already accused Francesca of being the Black Cat, and now Rosie."

"Eliza seems capable of anything," Nancy agreed.

"Writing curse notes, sabotaging elevators, and—who knows?—maybe even kidnapping. She could easily have planted the book in Francesca's shelf, and she hasn't explained the tar."

"She seems crazy enough to close down the school just because she's ticked off at it," George remarked.

Nancy frowned. "But there's no evidence that she can handle Tassie. I'd still like to track down Francesca and follow her. She's got this spacey way about her that I just don't trust."

"Why don't you follow Francesca while I trail Eliza?" George suggested.

Nancy grinned. "Good thinking, George. Let's do that. There's just one more thing."

"What?"

"Ms. Friedlander took Rosie Tsing aside after class yesterday, and Rosie looked pretty mad," Nancy said. "Maybe Ms. Friedlander was on her case for cheating. Eliza might be right about the grudge. I'd kind of like to find out more about Rosie."

The bell rang, and students filed out of the gym and into the locker room. Nancy followed Rosie inside.

The room was filled with steam. Nancy finally found Rosie in a far corner digging blue jeans out of her locker. "Can I talk to you for a moment?" Nancy asked her.

Rosie frowned up at her. "Now? I've got a lot of homework to finish before midwinter break, Ms.

Drew. I'd really like to get over to the library before the rest of the day is shot."

"It'll only take a moment," Nancy said, sitting down on the bench beside her. "I thought I should warn you that Eliza might try to bad-mouth you around the school. Does she have any evidence to support her story about your grudge?"

"Of course not!" Rosie said hotly. "She's such a liar—she just wants to spite people to get attention."

"So she lied when she hinted that you might be the Black Cat?" Nancy pressed.

"Totally!" Rosie said, her face red with outrage. "I may have had problems with Ms. Friedlander and everything, but I would never kidnap her!"

"What problems did you have with her?" Nancy asked.

Rosie lowered her eyes. "It's . . . true, I guess, that Ms. Friedlander accused me of cheating," Rosie stammered, stealing a guilty glance at Nancy before dropping her gaze once more. "She said I'd plagiarized an essay on 'The Black Cat' by a famous critic."

"Is that true?" Nancy asked.

"No! What do you take me for?" Rosie retorted.

"Then if she accused you of doing something you didn't do, wouldn't you be kind of mad at her?" Nancy asked.

"I was! No, I mean . . . I wasn't *that* mad," Rosie sputtered. "I wouldn't hold a grudge against her just because of her stupid accusations. After all, *I* know I didn't cheat." Straightening her shoulders, Rosie explained, "Anyway, the curses started before Ms. Friedlander and I argued yesterday. That fool Eliza doesn't know what she's talking about."

Nancy thanked Rosie for her time and left the gym with George and Kaleesha Jones.

When they were out of earshot of other girls, Nancy paused in the shadow of a fir tree and asked Kaleesha, "So what do you think about Rosie? Is there a chance she could really be guilty?"

"It's hard to believe that anyone I know would kidnap someone," Kaleesha said, shaking her head glumly. "But obviously someone around this place is guilty, and if I had to pick the most likely person, I'd vote for Rosie Tsing."

"Why?" Nancy asked, surprised.

"Because she's a straight-A senior who would do anything to be number one in the class," Kaleesha declared. "Right now I'm number one, and that drives Rosie nuts. She's always competing with me—whether I want to or not. I'm sure she erased my thesis."

"Do you think Rosie could have plagiarized a paper to get ahead?" Nancy asked.

"I wouldn't put it past her, and if Ms. Friedlander could prove it, Rosie would be in big trouble. Also, Rosie's family is hard up for money. Her parents owe the school so much tuition that she may not be able to graduate. The ransom money sure would solve that problem," Kaleesha said acidly.

George raised her eyebrows. "Sure would!"

"Well, I'll see you two later," Kaleesha said. "I'm off to the common room for some R and R. I'm still pretty shaken up about my thesis."

Nancy and George waved goodbye. The moment Kaleesha turned her back, George grabbed Nancy's arm. "Look behind us—at the gym!"

Nancy whirled toward the gym just in time to see Rosie slipping out a side door. Sneaking looks to either side of her, Rosie hurried around the far corner.

Without wasting a moment, Nancy and George ran after her. But just before they rounded the corner of the gym, footsteps pounded up fast behind them. Nancy's heart skipped a beat, but before she could turn, someone grabbed her shoulder from behind.

"Nancy, George—stop!" a girl's voice said.

Nancy and George whipped around—and instantly came face to face with Kaleesha.

"Mrs. Cook wants you guys now!" Kaleesha said breathlessly. "Something horrible has happened. Lila Van Voorhies is missing!"

11

A Cold Encounter

Nancy stared at Kaleesha, stunned. Then she and George took off toward Tower as fast as they could.

Once there, they found Mrs. Cook, ashen-faced, standing on the front portico and talking to the police.

"This is the most dreadful day in the history of Waverly Academy," she pronounced solemnly. "I never dreamed I'd be head of the school at a time like this—when a student may have been harmed."

Taking off her spectacles, she dabbed at her eyes with a hankerchief. Then she put them back on, straightened her shoulders, and bravely faced her listeners.

"What happened, Mrs. Cook?" Nancy asked, still feeling shocked.

"Lila didn't show up for her afternoon history class,"

91

Mrs. Cook explained. "I'd warned each teacher to keep a special watch on the girls who had received curse notes, because I thought they might be more vulnerable. So when Lila didn't come to class, her teacher grew worried. The police have just finished searching the school, but to no avail."

Mrs. Cook sighed, while George asked, "Did you find a note in her room, like the one addressed to Ms. Friedlander's parents?"

"There was no note on her bed," Mrs. Cook replied. "Instead, I received an e-mail on my computer repeating the demand for five million dollars to be delivered to the cat urn by five tomorrow. If no police are in sight and the delivery person leaves the scene promptly, then Lila and Ms. Friedlander will be returned safely and the curses will stop. But the Black Cat threatened even worse if the money doesn't get delivered. More girls will be harmed, and Waverly Academy will be doomed."

"What else did the note say? Will Lila and Ms. Friedlander just show up at the cat urn after the money's delivered?" Nancy asked.

"According to the note, an hour after the delivery, they'll appear at Tower."

Nancy put a comforting arm around the shaken headmistress. "I promise to get to the bottom of this mess as soon as possible," she whispered.

Mrs. Cook squeezed Nancy's hand. "I won't give up hope," she assured her.

While they were speaking, most of the police dispersed to comb the school grounds, search surrounding areas, and doublecheck all the Waverly buildings. But before Chief McGinnis went with them, he assured Mrs. Cook that they would ask at all the neighboring houses about the missing people.

As Nancy watched the police scatter across the lawn, she asked Mrs. Cook, "When was the last time anyone saw Lila?"

"In math class before lunch," she replied. "Some of her classmates told me that they all headed over to Tower for lunch, but no one remembers seeing Lila during lunch or later at free time."

"I'd like to find out whether any of my suspects have alibis for that time," Nancy said. "I saw both Francesca and Eliza during the last few minutes of free time. Who knows what they were doing before that?"

"Do they have alibis for when Ms. Friedlander disappeared?" George asked.

"I remember seeing both Francesca and Eliza at breakfast early—when Ms. Friedlander was there," Mrs. Cook mused. "About forty minutes passed between the time that they left the dining hall and the beginning of first period."

"Enough time to kidnap Ms. Friedlander and stash her somewhere," George remarked dryly.

Nancy told Mrs. Cook her suspicions about Rosie. "Was Rosie at breakfast early?" she asked.

Mrs. Cook tapped a finger on a porch column as she thought. "That's a good question. I don't remember seeing Rosie at breakfast," she finally said.

"Would it be okay if I searched Ms. Friedlander's apartment and Lila's room?" Nancy asked. "There's a chance I'll find some clue to the Black Cat there. I might discover a reason why someone would want to kidnap them."

"By all means, Nancy," Mrs. Cook said warmly. She took her key ring from her pocket and gave one of the keys to Nancy. "This is a master key for the apartments in Blue Jay," she explained.

"Thanks. I'll be careful with it," Nancy said, placing it in her coat pocket.

"And now I have to try to reach Edgar Van Voorhies, Lila's father," Mrs. Cook said grimly.

After Mrs. Cook had disappeared inside Tower, Nancy looked at her watch. "It's already three," she said to George. "From now until dinner is campus free time, when sports teams play other schools or clubs meet or kids just study. I might hold off on checking Lila's and Ms. Friedlander's rooms till after dinner. The police are probably there now, and this is a perfect time to follow Eliza and Francesca."

"You're right," George agreed. "If one of them is guilty, she'd probably do something suspicious now—before getting tied up with dinner and the play."

"We've lost track of Rosie," Nancy said, "but I'll get to work on Francesca right away."

"And I'll try to see what's up with Queen Eliza," George quipped.

Nancy headed toward Sparrow, in search of Francesca. As she hurried down the gravel path, she first passed Blackbird and then came to a place where the path ran alongside a stretch of woods. A narrow trail snaked off from the gravel path to cut through thick, dark trees.

A girl's soft laughter floated toward her from the woods. In the nick of time, Nancy scuttled under the branches of the nearest trees. The girl's laughter sounded closer. Nancy heard dead leaves and twigs being crunched by running footsteps.

Suddenly Rosie shot out from the trees on to the path, clutching a gym bag in her arms. Nancy crouched in the shadows as Rosie sneaked a quick look around her. Then she dashed down the path in the direction of Tower.

Nancy didn't waste a second. Careful not to make noise on the gravel, Nancy ran silently on the grass bordering the path, keeping Rosie just within her view. A few seconds later she passed Blackbird and then branched off from the main path onto a smaller one.

Drawing back against a tree, Nancy kept out of sight while Rosie sneaked a couple more glances around her. With only a few girls far away and minding their own business, Rosie sprinted toward a cement stairway at the back of Tower that led down to its basement level.

Nancy took off after her. After following Rosie inside the door at the bottom of the stairs, Nancy paused for a moment. She could barely see the basement boiler room around her as her eyes adjusted. A dim light flickered from a bare light bulb a half inch above her head. She stumbled forward, determined not to lose track of Rosie in the labyrinth of pipes. The room seemed huge—maybe even as big as the dining room above it, Nancy thought. Rosie's footsteps quickly grew fainter.

I've got to keep up, Nancy thought. But each way she turned, a pipe, like some sort of monstrous snake, blocked her way.

Nancy's pulse raced. She could no longer see the door to the outside. This is like some sort of nightmare maze, she thought, except there's no way out.

Nancy paused a moment to get her bearings. The basement was absolutely silent. Did Rosie find a way out? she wondered. Or is she lurking somewhere, waiting to attack me?

Just then Nancy heard a light pinging sound. Footsteps on metal, she thought. In the dim light she could barely make out an iron staircase in the corner of the room—and Rosie's sneakers already at the top. Ducking under a set of pipes, Nancy raced to follow her.

Once upstairs, Nancy found herself in another dimly

lit room—this one with two walk-in refrigerators off the main kitchen. Through an open door nearby, Nancy observed the hustle and bustle of a busy kitchen staff getting ready for dinner.

A hand clamped over Nancy's mouth. Before she could react, a plastic bag dropped over her head, and the world went dark.

Nancy struggled against whoever was pinning her arms from behind. But she was no match for the surprise attack. As the person dragged her backward, Nancy heard a door open and felt a blast of cold air. A rough arm pushed her to the floor.

Nancy pulled the bag off her head, then struggled to her feet, but not before the refrigerator door slammed shut, trapping Nancy in the pitch-black cold!

12

A Scream in the Night

Nancy took deep breaths of the frigid air. Then she yanked her penlight from her coat pocket and shone it around her icy prison.

Two feet in front of her was the door. Summoning all her strength, she pushed against it, but it didn't budge. Nancy knew it was illegal for the door not to open from the inside. It had to be wedged shut. Not a whisper of outside air was getting through, she realized. If the kitchen staff didn't need something from the refrigerator—and soon—she'd be in big trouble. Either hypothermia or suffocation would do her in before morning.

Nancy explored the back of the refrigerator with the penlight. Gallon bottles of milk and juice, large blocks of butter, and cartons of eggs were piled against the walls. Shivering, she pulled her coat tighter around her throat and considered her options.

It was near dinnertime, she knew, so someone in the kitchen might come looking for food.

The thought had barely flicked through her mind when heavy footsteps pounded toward the refrigerator. Yes! Nancy breathed. To her dismay, though, she heard the click of the other refrigerator latch opening. Pounding on her door, Nancy shouted at the top of her lungs, but the footsteps grew fainter.

Nancy sighed in frustration. If she could hear the person outside, why couldn't the person hear her? Her leg knocked against a jug of something—and an idea flashed through her mind. Shining her penlight on the jug, she saw that it was a gallon of milk.

Nancy grabbed the milk and took off the cap. Then she put her ear against the door to wait for more footsteps. A minute of silence went by.

The footsteps returned. Nancy pried at the seal at the bottom of the door with her car key and managed to make a tiny break. Then she poured the milk through it.

A thrill went through Nancy as she heard the footsteps hurrying toward her. Her idea was working!

The refrigerator door was opened. Light and warmth flooded toward Nancy as a young man wearing earphones attached to a pocket tape player stared in absolute astonishment at her.

"What . . . who are you?" he asked, stuffing his earphones into his shirt pocket alongside his tape player.

"I'm an intern here," Nancy replied, stepping out of the refrigerator and shutting the door behind her. "Someone locked me in."

The young man shot her a tentative smile, as if he wasn't sure whether she was joking. Then he said, "I did think it was odd that a chair was wedged under the handle."

"I've been shouting and banging on the door for a while," Nancy went on. "Didn't you hear me?"

"No, I'm sorry," the man said sheepishly. "I've had my music on loud. But the milk leaking from the bottom of the door sure got my attention," he added with a chuckle.

"Did you see a heavyset dark-haired girl carrying a gym bag?" Nancy asked, scanning the room. Her attacker must have hidden behind the door to the basement, waiting for her to come upstairs before grabbing her from behind.

"No," the man said, knitting his brow at Nancy's question. "Students aren't allowed in the kitchen. The only people I've seen around here are the cooks and the dishwashers, and none of them fits that description."

"Well, thank you for rescuing me," Nancy said gratefully.

"You're welcome," the young man said as he opened

the other refrigerator and retrieved several plastic bags filled with lettuce.

Nancy made her way through the kitchen and into the huge dining hall. The rectangular tables were already set with white tableclothes, silverware, glasses, and pitchers of water. The Gothic-style entryway was seething with girls waiting for the signal to enter and take their seats.

The dinner bell rang, and the girls burst into the dining hall, streaming toward Nancy as they scrambled for seats. Faculty members followed them to take their places as table heads.

Nancy started as she saw Rosie weaving through some chairs. Rosie's gaze rested on Nancy only briefly before flickering to the other students at her table. Hmm, Rosie barely seems to notice me, Nancy observed, surprised.

Nancy brushed by Eliza, who was surrounded by a group of girls complimenting her on her role as Guinivere. "You were sooo good last night, McBride," one girl crooned. "I'm going back for seconds tonight."

"I wish I had the nerve to step onstage the way you do," another girl said. "I mean, you're so confident."

"I'm planning a career in the theater," Eliza said smugly. "Look out, Broadway, here I come!"

Nancy rolled her eyes as she walked past. From a distance she caught sight of Francesca sitting at a corner table, staring dreamily around the room as if she were hypnotized by all the activity.

That girl looks as if she can barely find her way to

the dinner table, much less plan a series of curses and kidnappings, Nancy thought. Still, there was evidence against Francesca, she reminded herself, and her spaciness could be an act.

Nancy cast a look around for George, but she was nowhere to be seen. Maybe she's in the common room waiting for me to report back to her, Nancy thought. She headed out of the dining room into the hallway.

Sure enough, Nancy found George in the common room. "Eliza spent the whole afternoon here, playing cards with Lucy Slingluff. I'd have seen more action watching TV," George quipped. She glanced at Nancy curiously. "Did you have better luck with Francesca?"

Nancy sat down and told George about her encounter with Rosie. "Though I can't be totally sure that Rosie was the person who attacked me," Nancy added. "I mean, she didn't seem surprised to see me in the dining room or anything."

"But who else could it have been?" George asked. "Rosie went up the basement stairs just a minute ahead of you."

"She's definitely Suspect Number One at this point," Nancy assured her. "Still, I have no real evidence against her because I never saw the person who shut me in."

"Hey, guys, why aren't you in the dining room chowing down?" a familiar voice asked from the hallway.

"Bess!" Nancy and George said in unison, jumping up to greet her.

"What are you doing here?" Nancy asked, smiling.

"I couldn't take the suspense another minute," Bess said. "I've been curious all day to know whether you've caught the Black Cat, but since you guys haven't returned my zillions of phone messages, I had to take matters into my own hands and track you down."

"We haven't been home since this morning," Nancy said.

"Not even to get some of Hannah's cooking? I mean, boarding school food isn't exactly known for being gourmet," Bess remarked.

"We've been way too busy to think about food, Bess," George said, and grinned. "But since it seems to be tops in your mind, why don't you join us for dinner? I don't think one extra person will put a strain on the kitchen."

After updating Bess about the case, Nancy added, "It's great that you're here, Bess, because now there's a detective for each suspect. Once dinner's over, you can track Francesca, while George and I keep after Eliza and Rosie."

Bess shrugged. "Sounds okay to me. Francesca doesn't sound too dangerous, at any rate."

"I think Rosie's probably the most dangerous one," George remarked. "Though I risk death by boredom if I spend one more second with Eliza. Plus, she's going to be busy onstage all night."

"Let's meet back at Tower at midnight," Nancy suggested. "That'll give Eliza time after the play to do something—if she's going to."

George gave Nancy the thumbs-up sign, before leading the way into the dining room for dinner.

"This stuff's great!" Bess exclaimed, putting down her fork after finishing her baked Alaska. "I've changed my mind about boarding school food. I could spend my whole life here!" She looked regretfully at the remains of meringue and ice cream on Nancy's plate. "I can't believe you didn't finish yours."

"There's no time—Rosie's getting up to go," Nancy said, eyeing her quarry from across the room.

George stood up. "Here goes one more night of the Eliza McBride show," she groaned. "Do I get reimbursed for my pain and suffering?"

Nancy laughed. "When Eliza becomes a famous actor, maybe she'll reward you with her autograph. And now, guys, I've got to run, or I'll lose Rosie."

After pointing out Francesca to Bess, Nancy hurried to follow Rosie out of the room. Just as she rushed through the hallway of Tower, Rosie slipped out the front door.

Outside, Rosie rounded a bend in a path that veered off from Tower toward Einstein, the science lab. Nancy dashed down the portico stairs to catch up.

The night was dark with swirling clouds that made the sky look like a rolling ocean. But every few minutes the moon would shine down before a cloud covered it again. Nancy peered through the darkness ahead but saw nothing—not even a flicker of movement. Just as she lost all hope of finding Rosie, the moon flashed down on Rosie's short dark hair as she walked through the front door of Einstein.

Seconds later Nancy stood in the downstairs hallway of Einstein, peering into a lab where Rosie and Kaleesha Jones were writing notes next to some colored vials. Keeping the door cracked open, Nancy sat down cross-legged on the floor, drumming her fingers on her knee with impatience. Rosie may or may not be the Black Cat, Nancy knew, but nothing much was happening at this moment, except, surprisingly, that Rosie and Kaleesha were working together. Meanwhile Ms. Friedlander and Lila were in danger!

For half an hour Nancy watched the girls write. Finally they stood up to go. Nancy quickly ran out the front door and hid behind some nearby bushes. Maybe, Nancy hoped, Rosie will lead me to Ms. Friedlander and Lila *now*.

Nancy followed Kaleesha and Rosie as they returned to their rooms at Blackbird. Peering through a window into Rosie's first-floor room, Nancy crossed her fingers that Rosie would finally reward her with some evidence.

As Nancy watched, Rosie pressed a button on her computer to boot it up. Then she bent down to the gym bag at her feet. Nancy rose on her toes and stretched forward eagerly, straining to see what was inside.

Rosie sifted around inside the bag. She began to lift something out, but suddenly dropped the bag and left the room empty-handed.

Pressing forward, Nancy could just make out the bag on the floor, but whatever was inside it stayed hidden.

Where could Rosie be? Nancy wondered after five frustrating minutes had passed. She didn't want to leave her place at the window in case Rosie came back and dumped out the contents of her bag.

Just then a loud scream pierced the air. Nancy whipped around. The person screamed again—an anguished cry tearing through the cold night.

Nancy's heart pounded wildly in her chest. It sounded like Bess!

13

The Cat's Sharp Claws

Nancy didn't waste a moment. She took off toward the scream, which came from the woods near Blackbird. Gravel flew up around her as she sprinted down the path.

When she came to the thicket of trees that bordered the path, Nancy paused to locate the narrow trail in the darkness. Holding her penlight in front of her, she rushed down the trail.

Two hundred feet later a ramshackle shed appeared on her right.

The door burst open. To Nancy's amazement, Francesca stepped outside, wearing a guilty, stricken look on her face.

"Ms. Drew! I had no idea you'd be here!" she exclaimed.

"I didn't expect to see you, either," Nancy said, startled.

"I'm really sorry I'm out of my dorm this late," Francesca muttered. "You won't tell anyone, will you?"

"That depends. What are you doing here?" Nancy asked.

"I was afraid that Tassie might be hungry, so I came to feed him," Francesca said, wringing her hands. "Please don't tell Mrs. Cook you saw me here. I don't want to get in trouble."

"Did you hear a scream?" Nancy asked her.

Francesca knit her brow. "Hmm. I think I *did* hear a scream, but I didn't pay attention because Tassie seems to be missing." She looked at Nancy anxiously. "He could be in danger. He's such a cute cat. I hope he's okay."

Nancy couldn't bear to listen to Francesca another moment. She burst past her into the shed. Shining her penlight into each corner, she saw a few gardening tools, bowls of catfood and water, and a bag of mulch—but there was no sign of Bess or anyone else.

"He didn't come when I called," Francesca whispered behind her.

Nancy whirled around to face her. "What?" she asked impatiently.

"It's never happened before," Francesca went on, as if she hadn't heard Nancy. "Tassie always comes when I call him. I'm so worried that something awful has hap-

108

pened to him. Why else would he be ignoring me? Tassie? Tassie?" she called in her wispy voice.

"Did you see anyone around the shed tonight, Francesca?" Nancy asked. "A blond-haired girl, or anyone else?"

Francesca's eyes widened as she stared in shock at Nancy. "No. Why? Are you saying that someone could have stolen the cat? I mean, I guess Tassie *could* be a victim of all these curses, too. Why would he be different from a person?"

"Calm down, Francesca," Nancy said, glancing around to see if she could detect signs that Francesca and Bess had struggled. But everything inside the shed—the tools and gardening supplies—looked in order.

Frowning, Nancy studied Francesca, who was gazing at Nancy with a faraway expression in her big brown eyes.

Hmm, Nancy thought—it's kind of coincidental that Francesca is here at the same time that Bess may have screamed for help. And Bess was supposedly following her. Still, Francesca seems so clueless.

Nancy felt torn. On the one hand, she didn't want to let Francesca out of her sight. On the other, Bess wasn't here and Nancy *had* to find her.

After a moment's hesitation Nancy slipped by Francesca and continued down the path. Five minutes later Nancy passed through a gate that she guessed marked the edge of the school grounds. She came to a sidewalk lined by medium-size houses set behind hedges and trees. Tall street lamps overhung the road, which wound uphill and curved. Nancy looked around. There was no sign of Bess.

I've come too far, she thought, frustrated. Francesca must know more than she's letting on. Nancy turned around and raced back to Francesca, who was still calling Tassie in a plaintive voice from the doorway of the shed.

"Mrs. Cook wants to see you," Nancy told her.

Francesca started. "Wh . . . why?"

"Because you're out very late, Francesca, and she has some questions for you."

Francesca narrowed her eyes. "I thought you were on my side," she snapped. "You said you wouldn't tell her I was here."

"I never promised you that, Francesca," Nancy said firmly.

"This isn't fair," Francesca mumbled as she walked with Nancy back to Tower. "I'm the only person who cares about animals around here, and I get punished!"

Upstairs in Mrs. Cook's office, Nancy told Mrs. Cook and Detective Ghent about hearing Bess scream and finding Francesca. Detective Ghent immediately organized a search to canvass the school grounds and surrounding areas for Bess. He also had Nancy call Bess's home to make sure she hadn't returned.

Meanwhile, Francesca sat down in an armchair and crossed her arms grumpily as she pouted at Mrs. Cook. Detective Ghent and Nancy pulled up chairs next to her.

"It's after ten o'clock, Francesca," Mrs. Cook said. "You were wandering around in the woods near the gardener's toolshed, looking for a stray cat. You know that students aren't allowed outside after dark, unless they're on school-related business."

"I . . . I was coming from the library, when I decided to check on Tassie," Francesca stammered.

Mrs. Cook picked up the phone. "I'll just confirm your story with Mr. Tamiko, our librarian."

Francesca blanched. "No. I mean, I was on my way to the library when—"

"Bess Marvin may be missing," Detective Ghent said gravely. "Now tell us the truth. Did you hear a scream?"

Francesca swallowed. "Yes," she whispered.

"What time?" he pressed.

She shot the officer a frightened look. "I don't know," she wailed. "I never keep track of time."

Detective Ghent blew out his breath. "Let's try a different tack. I understand you own a book called *Famous American Short Stories*."

"Stop!" Francesca pleaded. "I already told Ms. Drew I've never seen that book—someone must be trying to frame me."

"That book is strong evidence against you, Francesca," Mrs. Cook said. "And you were near Bess when she disappeared. I understand she was following you."

"She had no reason to be!" Francesca cried. "I don't know anything about Bess Marvin or Ms. Friedlander

111

or Lila. I know nothing about the curse notes, except—"
She stopped abruptly, biting her lip.

"Except what?" Nancy prompted.

"Well, except maybe the tar."

"What do you know about the tar?" Detective Ghent asked. "Please tell us everything. I'm not sure you appreciate how serious this matter is."

Two tears slid down Francesca's cheeks as her story began to break down. "I know it's serious—three people are missing. But I promise I didn't hurt them. All I did was . . . was put the bucket of tar in Eliza's room yesterday." She shot a terrified look at Detective Ghent before dropping her face in her hands and breaking into sobs.

Mrs. Cook's stern expression softened as she leaned toward Francesca. "But why, dear?" she asked. "Why on earth did you do that?"

"Because I was mad at Eliza for accusing me of writing the curse notes!" Francesca cried. "I hoped the police would find the tar so she'd get blamed."

Nancy listened to Francesca's story and decided she was probably telling the truth about framing Eliza with the tar. First of all, not many people knew about the tar bucket in the closet. Also, Francesca wouldn't be likely to take blame for something she hadn't done.

Still, Nancy wasn't sure she believed that Francesca wasn't the Black Cat. She hadn't explained the book, and she was in the woods where Bess had disappeared while Bess was following her. Also, Francesca was obsessed with Catastrophe, and he was a black cat.

Nancy checked her watch. It was past time for the play to let out. Thanking Detective Ghent and Mrs. Cook, she excused herself to find George.

"Don't worry, Nancy. We'll do our best to find Bess," Detective Ghent assured her. Leaning toward her, he added in a low voice, "And we'll keep Francesca under constant surveillance—maybe she'll lead us to the others."

Nancy found George waiting for her downstairs in the common room. The moment Nancy told her about Bess, George sank back in her chair. "I'll bet the Black Cat is either Rosie or Francesca," George said shakily. "I hate to admit this, but after spending my evening with Eliza, I've decided she must be innocent."

"We can't use the tar against her anymore, either," Nancy said.

"Also, she was onstage when Bess disappeared," George said. "Then after the play let out, she went straight from the auditorium to her room in Blackbird. She was reading in bed when I came to find you a few minutes ago."

"I agree—Eliza's off the hook," Nancy said. "She may be weird and everything, but she can't be the Black Cat. That play gives her a pretty solid alibi. But Rosie wasn't in her room when Bess screamed, and Francesca was hanging out in the woods."

"But what could Francesca's motive be?" George asked. "Rosie's is tuition money, of course."

"And getting back at Ms. Friedlander for saying she cheated," Nancy added. "And I'm sure she would be thrilled to delete Kaleesha's thesis. Now she may be first in the class."

The grandfather clock in the hallway of Tower struck eleven. Nancy sighed, not wanting to leave Waverly until Bess was found. But she knew the police would work hard all night, doing everything possible to find her. "Let's go home, George," she said reluctantly. "First thing tomorrow I'm going to take a closer look at Lila and Ms. Friedlander's backgrounds. I have this feeling there's a link we're missing—something that will tell us who the Black Cat is."

"But what would the Black Cat want with Bess?" George wondered.

"Nothing," Nancy said. "Except that Bess may have been about to discover who she is."

The next morning Nancy, George, and Mrs. Cook rode the elevator up to the headmistress's office just as breakfast was letting out.

"Did the police find any hints about what happened to Bess?" Nancy asked her.

Mrs. Cook shook her head sadly. "No, I'm sorry to say."

Nancy's heart sank. Poor Bess—she was only trying

to help me solve this case, Nancy thought. I've got to find her.

"We'd like to investigate some dorm rooms while the girls are in class," Nancy said to Mrs. Cook. "I know the police have already searched Lila's and Ms. Friedlander's rooms, but I'd like to look for myself."

"And I want to check out Rosie's gym bag," George chimed in.

"Please—do whatever is necessary," Mrs. Cook said, wringing her hands. "I was hoping we'd have it all sewn up by now, but it's only grown worse. And I want to remind you both that school closes today at noon for midwinter break. All the students and faculty will be leaving. I, of course, will stay here until the Black Cat is found."

"After school gets out," Nancy said, "the Black Cat will go to the hideout to wait for the ransom drop-off at five o'clock. Maybe the victims will be at that hideout."

"Maybe," Mrs. Cook said. "If only we knew where it was."

After their meeting with Mrs. Cook, Nancy and George headed over to Blackbird to search Rosie's and Lila's rooms. Lila's room was on the first floor, Nancy found, on the opposite side of the dorm from Rosie's.

Stepping inside Lila's neatly kept room, Nancy headed for her desk to search for personal letters or a diary—anything that would have information about her background.

Nancy opened the top drawer. Inside was a stack of

letters held together by a rubber band. Nancy picked up the first letter. It was addressed to Lila with Edgar Van Voorhies's return address in the upper lefthand corner. He was Lila's father, Nancy remembered.

The skin on Nancy's neck suddenly prickled. Someone was behind her—she could feel it. She whipped around.

A black-cloaked figure in a huge cat mask with red eyes and vampire teeth loomed before her.

Shock flooded through Nancy as the figure grabbed her. Ten sharp masonry nails stuck out crazily from its leather gloves like cat's claws.

Nancy cringed in the apparition's grip. With its nails digging against her cheek, the figure growled, "Drop that letter, or I'll rip you to shreds!"

14

Scooter's Revenge

Nancy's arms were pinned to her sides, and she was forced to drop the letter. Tightening its grip, the Cat dragged her toward the bedroom door. Nancy struggled to kick the creature's legs, but she couldn't get her balance. She opened her mouth to scream.

The Cat jabbed its nails against her throat. "One peep, honey, and you're history," it hissed.

The Cat opened the door and shoved Nancy on to the hallway floor. Then it slammed the door and locked it.

Nancy clambered to her feet. In an instant she unfastened the barrette from her hair and poked it into the lock. The door sprang open.

Scanning the room cautiously, Nancy stepped inside, ready to use karate at any moment. But the win-

117

dow was open, and the Black Cat and Lila's letters were gone.

Nancy checked the closet—she didn't want the Cat to trick her and ambush her from behind. The moment she saw it was empty, Nancy ran to the window and looked outside.

On her left the gravel path curved by the woods where she'd found Francesca the night before. Nancy could see the trail cutting into the trees about fifty yards away.

Nancy did a double take. Some pine boughs next to the trail were swaying, as if someone had recently brushed by them.

Nancy scrambled through the window and leaped to the ground. Seconds later she was racing down the trail at top speed.

Something tells me that Tassie isn't the only black cat who hangs out in that gardener's shed, Nancy thought.

Nancy willed herself to run faster, her breath forming white plumes in the cold air. The moment she saw the shed, she crept up to it quietly and peeked through a broken window.

Nancy's heart sank at the sight of the empty room. Still, Nancy was sure the Black Cat had turned down this trail. It couldn't have ventured toward the school all dressed up like that, she reasoned. Also, someone had definitely brushed against the boughs of those trailside trees.

Nancy left the shed and continued along the trail

until she came to the street. Scanning it up and down, Nancy saw no one.

Nancy felt something cold and wet on her face. She blinked up at the sky. Snow!

Flakes were dancing through the air. As Nancy watched, the snow began to make webs of white on the greenish brown lawns and soften the harsh metallic colors of parked cars.

Nancy headed back down the trail, determined to continue her search of Lila's room until she found a clue. Obviously, she reasoned, there are some things about Lila that the Black Cat doesn't want me to know.

After twenty minutes of combing through Lila's possessions and finding nothing that seemed important, Nancy gave up. It was time to investigate Ms. Friedlander's apartment in Blue Jay, she decided.

As she passed the portico of Tower on her way to Blue Jay, George dashed down the stairs and grabbed her arm.

"Where have you been, Nancy?" she asked. "The minute I finished searching Rosie's stuff, I looked for you in Lila's room, but you were gone. I've been waiting here ever since, hoping I'd run into you. I was getting worried."

Nancy told George about the cat figure.

"I'm glad you're okay," George told her. "But listen to this. I searched Rosie's gym bag, and guess what I found on top of some clothes?"

"What?" Nancy asked excitedly.

"An English paper written by a boy named Chris Kramer who goes to Granger Academy."

"Mrs. Cook mentioned that school to me," Nancy said. "It's a boys' school that Waverly girls have proms with."

"Well, Chris got a A on his paper," George declared, "and I think he sold it to Rosie. See, when I checked out her calendar, there was a note on it that said, 'After gym: buy *it* from CK.' "

"Wow!" Nancy exclaimed. "Then Ms. Friedlander is right. Rosie is a cheater. But that also means she's probably off the hook for the kidnappings. She was acting suspicious because she knew she'd cheated."

George nodded her head in agreement. "She must have been in the woods to get the paper from Chris, not for stuff like sneaking food to Ms. Friedlander and Lila or planning another curse. She still could have attacked you in the kitchen, though. She might have thought you'd seen her buying the paper from Chris."

"Maybe," Nancy said. "But that leaves us with Francesca as the only strong candidate for the Black Cat. Would you mind trailing her, George, while I check Ms. Friedlander's apartment for clues?"

"Sure. Francesca's probably in some class now—I'll ask Mrs. Cook. Don't worry. I'll keep tabs on her every move."

"Thanks," Nancy said. "See you later."

Nancy hurried toward Blue Jay in the thickening snow. Once inside Ms. Friedlander's living room, Nancy stepped beyond the police crime tape, knowing they'd already dusted for fingerprints. She crossed over to Ms. Friedlander's desk.

Hunting through the top two drawers, she found nothing but pencils, pens, and stationery. In the bottom drawer, a stack of paper and manila folders made a suspicious bulge, as if something was hidden there.

Nancy dug down—and found a laptop computer underneath. Why was this thing hidden? she wondered as she drew it out. Maybe Ms. Friedlander just didn't use it anymore. Or maybe the police had shoved it in there when they were searching.

Placing the computer on the desk, Nancy turned it on and clicked onto the file icon. About twenty files popped into view, most of which were unimportant letters. But there was a file called "Scooter's Revenge" that piqued Nancy's curiosity.

That's a weird name for a file, she thought as she opened it.

A blank screen flashed into view. Disappointed, Nancy moved to a nearby bookshelf and scanned the shelves for information. Among the regular hardcover and paperback books was a beat-up green leather binder. Pulling it out, Nancy saw that it was an old photograph album.

Nancy sat down and flipped through the pages. Most of the pictures were snapshots of Ms. Friedlander as a child and teenager. But in one picture, a happy-looking Ms. Friedlander was sitting on a sofa with a middle-aged couple. Grinning from ear to ear, she held a big black cat on her lap. A caption underneath the picture read: "Me with Mom, Dad, and Scooter."

So Scooter was a black cat, Nancy observed. But why would he need to be avenged?

Nancy remembered that Ms. Friedlander's parents were dead. Ms. Friedlander herself couldn't be much older than twenty-five or six, Nancy judged. It's unusual that both her parents would have died so young.

Nancy shut the album and reached for the phone on Ms. Friedlander's desk. George had discovered that Ms. Friedlander was from Portland, Oregon, Nancy remembered. Why had Ms. Friedlander applied for a job at a school so far from home?

Mrs. Cook answered her phone in a defeated tone so unlike her usual self, Nancy thought. When Nancy asked her about Ms. Friedlander coming all the way to River Heights from Oregon, Mrs. Cook said, "Most of our teachers are from the River Heights or Chicago area. But a few do come from farther away. Angela Friedlander answered an ad I put in a national magazine. She had three years of experience teaching at a coed school in Oregon, and she came highly recommended."

Nancy told Mrs. Cook about Ms. Friedlander's black cat called Scooter. "I wonder what 'Scooter's Revenge' could mean?" she added. "It's pretty coincidental that a victim of the Black Cat owned one herself. I wonder if Lila had one, too. Maybe that's what Lila and Ms. Friedlander have in common."

"Wait!" Mrs. Cook exclaimed. "That reminds me. Lila and Angela *do* have something in common. I told George yesterday that Lila was from Los Angeles. But her family moved from Portland to Los Angeles two years ago. It's probably just a coincidence, Nancy, but two of the Black Cat's victims were originally from Portland."

"That may not be a coincidence," Nancy said uneasily. "Do you still have the names of Ms. Friedlander's references?"

"Yes, there was the headmaster of the school where she used to teach, and also a family friend named Ned O'Leary."

After copying down the names and numbers, Nancy thanked Mrs. Cook and hung up. Nancy first called Mr. Fox, the headmaster of Ms. Friedlander's previous school, but when she learned he was out for the day, she immediately telephoned Mr. O'Leary.

"Hello?" he said on the first ring.

After introducing herself, Nancy told Mr. O'Leary

that she was calling from Waverly Academy to update its faculty files.

"Can you tell me about Angela Friedlander?" she asked.

"You guys just called me about her last summer," he said gruffly. "What more do you need to know?"

"On Ms. Friedlander's job application, she says that her parents are deceased," Nancy said, pretending to read information from Ms. Friedlander's school files. "Is that true?"

"Yes, Angela's parents died two years ago in a car accident," he replied. "The poor girl."

"How well did you know her?" Nancy asked.

"Her family lived next door to me. She grew up in that house. But what does all this have to do with her job at your school?" he asked warily.

"She's been the victim of some pranks," Nancy said, not wanting to worry Mr. O'Leary with the whole truth. "We're trying to find out more information about the person who's been doing them. Angela's background might give us some clues."

"I don't see why she can't answer you herself," Mr. O'Leary said in a cranky tone. "But since you've got me on the phone, I'll help you if I can."

"Why did Angela leave Portland?" Nancy asked.

"She was done in by the accident," Mr. O'Leary said. "She not only lost her parents, but her beloved cat, Scooter, died in that car wreck, too."

"He did?" Nancy asked, her mind clicking away.

"Well, he was just a cat, but she took his death hard—and her parents', too, of course," he added quickly.

"What happened? Did another car run into them?" Nancy asked.

"They veered off the road into a tree in broad daylight. "No other car was around, and the roads were perfectly dry."

"Was there something wrong with the car?" Nancy asked.

"No," Mr. O'Leary said. "It's a long story. You see, a few months before the accident, the Friedlanders had lost most of their money in bad stock transactions. They were devastated to find themselves suddenly close to bankruptcy, and Matthew—Mr. Friedlander—started to suffer bad fainting spells. I always suspected that the accident may have resulted from one of these spells—and I shared my suspicions with Angela."

"So maybe Angela blamed her parents' deaths—and her cat's—on the bad investments," Nancy guessed.

"I think so," Mr. O'Leary agreed.

Nancy thought for a moment, then asked, "What kind of stocks did Mr. Friedlander buy? I mean, how did he invest his money so unwisely?"

"He took the advice of his stockbroker. You can be

sure he never forgave that bozo. Now, if you've no more questions, Ms. Drew, I'll be on my way."

"Wait!" Nancy said. "I have one more question." She drew a deep breath and asked, "Do you know the name of Mr. Friedlander's adviser?"

"I certainly do," he declared. "It's Edgar Van Voorhies."

15

Snowbound!

Nancy's heart skipped a beat when she heard the name.

"Thank you so much, Mr. O'Leary," she said. "You've been very helpful."

Nancy hung up, then immediately called Mrs. Cook. "Hi, it's Nancy," she said, when Mrs. Cook picked up the phone. "I think I know what's happening."

"You do?" Mrs. Cook said. "Please tell me everything."

Nancy told Mrs. Cook the story she'd learned from Mr. O'Leary. "I think that Ms. Friedlander made up all the curses," she added. "I think she made this elaborate plot to achieve one simple goal."

"Kidnapping Lila?" Mrs. Cook cut in.

"That's right," Nancy said. "All along her goal was to

kidnap Lila—partly for revenge against Mr. Van Voorhies and partly to get back her own family's money."

"Lila's father is a wealthy stockbroker," Mrs. Cook told her. "Angela must know he can afford to give up five million dollars for his daughter's safety. He's on his way to River Heights right now with the ransom money. His plane is due in at two o'clock."

"I'm so glad," Nancy said. "Even though I'm almost positive that the Black Cat is Ms. Friedlander, Lila and Bess are still in lots of danger. We've got to give Ms. Friedlander the money so she won't harm them."

"I wonder why she went to all that trouble making up curses?" Mrs. Cook mused. "Why not just kidnap Lila?"

"Because she wanted to seem less suspicious by getting kidnapped herself," Nancy said. "I'll bet she wanted everyone to think that some student had gone crazy, writing these random curses and stuff."

"It's as if she's enjoyed this Black Cat revenge act as a way to soothe her grief about her parents and Scooter," Mrs. Cook said.

Nancy felt a chill at the thought of Ms. Friedlander's plot. She really does mean business, Nancy thought. Nancy only hoped that Bess and Lila were okay.

Nancy's mind turned to the curse notes. "I'll bet those curse notes were saved in the file called

'Scooter's Revenge,' " she remarked to Mrs. Cook. "Ms. Friedlander probably deleted the master note before she disappeared so that no one would find it and discover what was going on."

"Nancy, you're a genius for figuring this all out," Mrs. Cook said. "I'm absolutely positive you're right— everything you said makes perfect sense. I'm going to speak with the police about your suspicions. They can catch the Cat when she comes to the cemetery to pick up her money."

"I'll be with them to help out," Nancy declared.

"I don't want you to take too many risks," Mrs. Cook said. "You've already exposed yourself to more danger than I'd like. In fact, I think you should get out of Angela's apartment ASAP. It's not safe for you to be there alone. Why don't you round up George and hole up in my office until Mr. Van Voorhies and the police show up? Then you and George can ride in a squad car to the cemetery with them—if you promise you won't get out."

Nancy smiled. She knew she couldn't make that promise if Bess and Lila needed her. "I'll come right over to Tower," she said.

"Please do, Nancy," Mrs. Cook urged. "The campus is deserted, and we've got a crazy woman on the loose."

"Has everyone left for vacation already?" Nancy asked, checking her watch. It was almost noon.

"Yes. Most of the students and faculty cleared out

earlier because of the blizzard forecast for this afternoon."

"I'll see you in a minute," Nancy promised, and hung up the phone.

After locking the apartment, Nancy rushed outside. Thick swirling flakes hid the trees and buildings behind a screen of white. The school grounds were deserted, Nancy noticed, as she struggled through the driving snow toward the vague gray outline of Tower.

A dark-hooded figure suddenly loomed a few feet ahead of her, blocking her way. Nancy stiffened, ready to defend herself.

"Have you been in Ms. Friedlander's apartment all this time?" a familiar voice asked.

"George! Why aren't you inside?" Nancy asked.

"I was on my way to find you," George replied. "I'd been waiting for you in the common room to tell you my discovery, but you took so long that I wanted to make sure you weren't buried in a snowdrift."

"Let's get inside," Nancy said, taking George's arm.

Once inside Tower, George pushed back her hood and said, "I'd been tracking Francesca, and she and Rosie left in an airport shuttle van about forty-five minutes ago. So I went to Francesca's room to do some snooping, and look what I found in the back of her bureau drawer."

She whipped out a rubber stamp from her pocket and pressed it into the palm of her hand. Sure enough, a faint image of a black cat appeared on her skin. "It's the Black Cat of the curse notes!" George exclaimed. "Francesca's obviously guilty. I'll bet she just went to the airport to fool everyone. She'll be sneaking back to get her money later, I'm sure. I just hope Bess and Lila are somewhere warm during this storm."

Studying George's hand, Nancy said, "It's the Black Cat image, all right. The stamp must have been planted in Francesca's room along with the book."

"Planted?"

Nancy nodded as she led George down the hall. While they waited for the elevator, Nancy told George what she'd discovered about Ms. Friedlander.

"I can't believe it!" George said when Nancy had finished. "The Black Cat was Ms. Friedlander all along?"

"I'm ninety-nine percent positive," Nancy said, smiling. "Now we've just got to find her—and rescue Lila and Bess."

As the elevator creaked upward, Nancy felt hopeful. Even though she knew their opponent was dangerous and Lila's and Bess's fates were still unresolved, Nancy couldn't help feeling that discovering the Cat's identity had been half the battle.

But the moment Nancy and George stepped into Mrs. Cook's office, Nancy knew that something terrible had happened.

"Nancy, George—I'm so glad you're here!" Mrs.

Cook said, jumping out of her seat. In a distraught tone, she went on, "I've just learned that the River Heights airport is closing because of the snow. Lila's father's plane is being diverted to St. Louis. But the ransom money is due at five o'clock!"

"Have you told the police?" Nancy asked.

"I was just on the phone with headquarters," Mrs. Cook replied. "There was a change of shift when the snow began, but no one from the new shift has reported to me because of snow emergencies. How are we going to rescue Lila and Bess?"

"The police will show up before five, won't they?" Nancy asked.

"The dispatcher said they'd try. The roads may be impassable," Mrs. Cook said. "But if they don't, we're supposed to stuff a manila envelope with newspaper and take it to the cemetery. After Angela picks it up, we're to follow her and hope she leads us to her captives."

"But she'll probably check the envelope right away to see if all the money's there," Nancy observed, frowning. Then she forced herself to smile at Mrs. Cook. "Don't worry," she added bravely. "George and I can handle things. We'll take the envelope to the cemetery and wait for Ms. Friedlander to come. We'll follow her from there."

"And cross our fingers that she'll lead us to Lila and Bess," George added.

Mrs. Cook frowned. "I just don't like the idea of you two girls facing Angela alone."

"We can do it," Nancy said. "After all, it'll be two against one."

At four-fifteen Nancy and George were ready to go. They'd spent a couple of anxious hours in Mrs. Cook's office. Nancy placed the manila envelope they'd filled with paper inside a waterproof bag, then stepped into the elevator.

"Goodbye, girls," Mrs. Cook said, hugging them as they left. "And good luck."

Earlier Mrs. Cook had given them directions to the cemetery. Now, as they made their way past Catastrophe's shed, through the knee-deep drifting snow, Nancy was glad that she and George had been able to borrow extra clothes and heavy boots from one of the rooms in Tower.

Soon the trail opened onto the street, where cars and houses were bundled in white. Yellow lamplight glowed like friendly beacons from the houses, but Nancy couldn't feel cheered by it.

The girls began to trudge uphill. As they rounded a bend, the houses thinned out, and the hill grew steeper. Slipping on the snow as they climbed, Nancy and George pushed on through the darkness. Finally Nancy spotted the cemetery gate at the top of the hill, lit up by a street lamp.

"Ouch!" George said, grimacing as she slipped. She grabbed her ankle and slumped down in the snow. "I think I just twisted my ankle, Nancy. You go on."

"No way, George. I can't leave you alone in this blizzard. Here—lean on me."

"But I'll slow you down," George moaned as Nancy grabbed her under her arms. With Nancy's help, George struggled to her feet. Then Nancy dragged her through the cemetery gate.

The gravestones looked like various sizes of marshmallows, Nancy thought. She glanced around desperately as the wind blasted flakes into her face. How was she ever going to find the cat-shaped urn under all this snow?

George groaned, shifting more of her weight onto Nancy. "All these mounds look alike," George muttered. "I'll just sit on one and wait for you. I hope he or she doesn't mind," she added, gingerly brushing snow off a gravestone.

"You can't stay here, George," Nancy said. "There's no shelter." Through the thick curtain of snow, she spotted a large houselike structure about twenty feet away. "Let's see what this is."

Supporting George, Nancy moved toward the structure. Soon Nancy could make out a round marble building with a portico and a padlocked iron door. Classical columns lined the front. "It's a mausoleum," Nancy remarked. "But at least there's shelter for you here on this porch."

"I'd feel safer out in the storm," George said darkly. "I mean, think what's behind that door."

Nancy checked her watch. It was five of five. "It's almost time," she said urgently. "I've got to find that cat-shaped urn. Just stay here, George, so at least I know you're okay."

George sat down on the portico, hugging her knees to her chin. She cast a doubtful look at the mausoleum's door. "I guess I'll be okay," she muttered, "as long as you're careful, Nancy."

Nancy gave George the thumbs-up sign, trying to feel as confident as she could. Then she slogged onward through the snow.

But as she took stock of the white mounds, which all looked alike in the snow, Nancy began to feel discouraged. Despite the street lamp at the cemetery gate, Nancy couldn't see more than ten feet in front of her. The cat urn could be anywhere.

Trudging along, Nancy suddenly jolted to attention. Ahead was a grave marker without any snow on it.

Weird, Nancy thought, moving closer to investigate.

Relief flooded through her. The sculpture was a carved stone cat, and inside the cat's shoulders was an empty space—for plants or flowers, Nancy assumed. This must be the cat-shaped urn!

Nancy glanced around. Snow-covered graves, a clump of yew bushes, and a tree loomed at the edge of her vision. Her skin prickled. Ms. Friedlander must have brushed the snow off the urn so I could find it, Nancy reasoned. She's probably even watching me right now.

Nancy stuffed the envelope inside the urn and ducked behind a tree. Minutes later a dark, hooded figure appeared through the storm and headed for the urn. Reaching inside, it quickly took out the envelope.

The figure turned to go. Nancy jumped from behind the tree, ready to follow. But at that instant, the figure stopped and looked around, as if checking to make sure no one was around.

Adrenaline shot through Nancy. She sees me! She's going to run! Nancy thought.

Before the figure could escape, Nancy rushed up and pushed it to the ground.

The hood fell back. Ms. Friedlander's hazel eyes glared up at Nancy from behind her glasses.

"Take me to Bess and Lila!" Nancy demanded as she pinned her down.

"Never!" Ms. Friedlander cried, thrusting Nancy aside. She yanked something out of her pocket.

Nancy's veins turned to ice. It was a butcher knife. She jumped away.

Ms. Friedlander leaped up after her. With her knife clutched in her hand, Ms. Friedlander chased Nancy toward a row of graves.

Nancy ran as fast as she could. But the thick snow made progress almost impossible. She felt as if she were in a nightmare, running for her life when her legs wouldn't move.

Ms. Friedlander's heavy footsteps grew closer, and Nancy sneaked a look behind. Ms. Friedlander, her knife held high, was only about five feet away!

Nancy sprinted forward. The graves were like a maze, she thought—one looked exactly like another. With the flakes stinging her face and her boots filled with snow, Nancy grew disoriented.

The ground began to slope downward. In a flash of horror Nancy stared ahead. Five feet away the white blanket of snow ended in total darkness. A cliff!

Nancy whirled around to face Ms. Friedlander. Like a charging bull, Ms. Friedlander ran at her.

She's going to knock me off the cliff, Nancy thought, jumping aside to avoid her.

But Ms. Friedlander caught Nancy and shoved her toward the edge of the precipice. A small scraggly tree jutted out at a forty-five-degree angle.

Just as Ms. Friedlander was about to push her over the brink, Nancy struggled out of her grasp and slid to the ground. Grabbing the tree, she straddled it with her legs. The abyss stretched beneath her on either side.

But Ms. Friedlander's momentum kept her going. She skidded to the edge of the cliff as she lost her balance.

Screaming in panic, Ms. Friedlander frantically tried to keep herself from falling. Like a fish flopping on the bank of a stream, she rolled onto her stomach and grabbed a tree root next to Nancy.

"Give me your hand, Nancy!" she begged as the scrawny root loosened in her grip. Her legs dangled over the brink as she looked up helplessly. "If I die, how will you ever find Bess and Lila?"

16

A Lucky Catastrophe

"Tell me where they are, and I'll help you!" Nancy said.

Ms. Friedlander glanced into the void below her before returning her gaze to Nancy. "I don't need your pathetic help, after all, Nancy Drew. I've seen this cliff in the daylight, and there's a chance I'll survive the fall. But I'll never tell you where Lila Van Voorhies is—her father ruined my family."

"Just give up," Nancy urged, holding tight to her tree to keep balanced as the terrifying darkness yawned up at her.

"You'll never find them, Nancy," Ms. Friedlander chortled. "They'll die a slow death of starvation locked in their nameless prison!"

Nancy's heart raced as Ms. Friedlander spoke her

dreadful words, but she forced herself to calm down. Somehow, she had to capture Ms. Friedlander alive.

Holding tight to her tree, Nancy extended her hand toward the teacher. "Give me your hand," she said evenly. "If we're careful, I can get you up."

In a flash Ms. Friedlander lunged up at Nancy and tried to grab her arm. She's going to pull me down! Nancy thought, recoiling. But before Ms. Friedlander could touch her, three shadowy figures appeared through the snow at the top of the cliff. One was leaning on another.

"Who's that?" Ms. Friedlander asked, freezing. Her eyes filled with panic.

Nancy felt like cheering. Through the whirling snow, she exchanged looks of relief with George, Lila, and Bess.

In one swift motion Lila and Bess reached down and gripped Ms. Friedlander under her arms. Then they hauled her to safety. While George and Lila kept Ms. Friedlander's arms pinned behind her, Bess helped Nancy back up to the firm snow-covered ground.

"Where did you guys come from?" Nancy asked, astonished. "And how in the world did you find me?"

"One question at a time," Bess said. "First, George saved Lila and me. We were shut inside that mausoleum where she'd taken shelter."

"The minute I was alone on the porch, I heard this muffled noise inside," George explained, using her belt

140

to tie Ms. Friedlander's wrists behind her back. "And since I'm not the type to believe in ghosts," she added, with a playful look at Bess, "I pried the hinges off the door with my bike key. They were rusty and about to fall apart anyway."

"You can't imagine how happy Lila and I were to see George instead of Ms. Friedlander!" Bess exclaimed.

Meanwhile, Ms. Friedlander struggled against George and Lila as they secured the belt. "Your father killed my family!" she spat at Lila. "You don't deserve to live!"

Lila stared into the hate-filled eyes of her kidnapper. Then she coolly turned her gaze to Nancy. "About your second question, Nancy," Lila went on. "Ms. Friedlander had threatened to throw me and Bess off the cliff if we ever tried anything funny. We guessed she might try to do the same thing to you, so we immediately rushed over here."

"Are you guys okay?" Nancy asked, concerned. "Did she hurt you?"

"We're fine," Lila said. "It was cold and scary in that place, but at least there was no mummy or anything in there with us."

Bess shuddered. "But we never even knew we were inside a crypt till George rescued us. See, Ms. Friedlander put a rag soaked with chloroform to our noses in the woods near school—at different times, of course.

When we each woke up, we were in this weird dark place. We had no clue what it was."

"You guys must be starving," Nancy commented.

"Ms. Friedlander brought me dinner last night," Lila said. "Then after Bess came, we both got breakfast and lunch."

"We could have done with better desserts," Bess quipped. "Soggy graham crackers just didn't cut it."

"And you got through all that snow on your hurt ankle, George?" Nancy asked, impressed.

George shrugged. "The cemetery's not as big as the blizzard makes it seem—and Bess's shoulder made a comfortable pillow."

Bess made a face at her cousin, while Nancy urged, "Let's get Ms. Friedlander back to Tower, guys, before this snow buries us. We can talk more once we're there. Here, George, you lean on me."

With Nancy and George on one side of Ms. Friedlander and Lila and Bess on the other, they made sure that the teacher couldn't escape. Huddled against the wind, they slogged their way down the winding road to the trail that led back to Waverly.

Once they were safely inside Tower, the four girls escorted Ms. Friedlander up to Mrs. Cook's office in the elevator.

"You're safe!" Mrs. Cook exclaimed, leaping up from the chair behind her desk. She rushed over to the four girls and embraced them.

After greeting Mrs. Cook and assuring her that they were well, the girls immediately got to work tying Ms. Friedlander to a chair with strong rope. Then Mrs. Cook picked up the phone to call the St. Louis airport, where Lila's father was waiting out the storm.

After she gave him the good news and Lila spoke to him, she called police headquarters and told Chief McGinniss that Ms. Friedlander had been captured. He promised he'd send a squad car over as soon as the storm allowed.

Mrs. Cook hung up, and she and the girls sat down to question Ms. Friedlander.

"We know why you kidnapped Lila," Nancy said. "But why did you take Bess?"

"Your nosy friend was in the wrong place at the wrong time," Ms. Friedlander snarled. "I was trying to lure Tassie into a cat carrier near the shed where Francesca feeds him. I needed him to do another curse against Nancy, who was getting way too curious for my liking. But Bess caught me in the act. She put two and two together and figured out I was the Black Cat. I had to get her out of the way."

"I was following Francesca," Bess explained, "but I didn't see her go inside the shed. I ran by it and saw Ms. Friedlander."

"And you carried the girls all the way up that long hill to the cemetery?" Mrs. Cook asked.

"I drove them in my car," Ms. Friedlander replied.

"I'd already discovered the mausoleum when I was making plans to kidnap Lila. I noticed it wasn't locked, so I supplied my own padlock."

"Did you plant the book and the stamp in Francesca's bedroom?" George asked.

"Clever of me, huh?" Ms. Friedlander said proudly. "That girl's attachment to Tassie made her a perfect suspect."

"But how did Tassie get into your desk drawer?" Nancy asked, remembering the curse note that Ms. Friedlander made for herself.

"The drawer was open when I arrived before class, and he was sleeping in it. I had some extra curse notes in my purse, so I thought of doing one against myself. I sneaked the note in beside him and then shut the drawer. He didn't get upset until I opened it again."

"You sure were busy organizing all those curses, Angela," Mrs. Cook commented. "Swapping Ramona's CD, putting tar on Lucy's sneakers and cutting Eliza's hair, swapping Lila's eyeglasses, and deleting Kaleesha's thesis—you must have worked hard planning all those things."

"Yes, but I had fun," Ms. Friedlander said gleefully. "I liked upsetting people, because *my* life had been ruined. I wanted to make people miserable like me."

"How did you figure out that I was investigating the case?" Nancy asked.

"By eavesdropping at Mrs. Cook's stairway door when

she first phoned you, Nancy," Ms. Friedlander explained. "I was thinking of putting a curse on her, but when I discovered she was in her office, I listened in on her instead."

"I assume you pushed me inside the refrigerator," Nancy said. "But what were you doing in the kitchen, anyway?"

"Getting food to sneak to Lila," Ms. Friedlander said. "I hid behind the cellar door when I heard footsteps on the stairs because I didn't want to be seen. But when you showed up right after Rosie, it was a perfect opportunity to get you out of my way."

"You almost got her out of the way when you sabotaged the elevator," Mrs. Cook said sternly.

"That metal saw I found in the basement didn't work all that well," Ms. Friedlander said regretfully. "If it had, I wouldn't be in this mess right now."

"What were you doing in Lila's room, dressed up in the cat costume?" Nancy asked.

"I wanted to search it to make sure there was no clue linking us," Ms. Friedlander replied. "I knew you were too good a detective not to check out her room, Nancy. When I heard you come in, I jumped into the closet to plan a surprise attack. Then I grabbed all of Lila's letters just in case there was evidence in them against me." She threw Nancy a scathing look. "And isn't it obvious why I dressed up? So I wouldn't be seen, of course. I mean, I had to stay in character—Angela Friedlander was supposed to be missing."

Mrs. Cook sat down behind her desk and glared at Ms. Friedlander. "When the police come, they'll place you under arrest. I hope you realize how serious the charges are against you."

"Let them lock me up!" Ms. Friedlander said defiantly. "Nothing can harm me as badly as Edgar Van Voorhies has already harmed my family."

"Your financial problems weren't my father's fault," Lila shot back. "Sure, he had high hopes for that stock, but he recommended that your dad put just a small percentage of his money into it because he knew it was risky. But your dad wanted to get rich quick, so he invested a big chunk of his money in it. After the stock bombed, my dad had to move to Los Angeles to escape your dad's unfair accusations, which were totally ruining his business."

Straining against the rope that held her, Ms. Friedlander barked, "You wretch! Can't you understand? I'll never see my parents or Scooter again!"

"We feel for you, Angela," Mrs. Cook cut in. "You suffered an awful tragedy. But you can't take out your grief on innocent people, even if you believe they're guilty. The law is there to do that, just as it will prosecute you for harming Lila, Bess, and all the other students here at Waverly."

Glancing at the girls, Mrs. Cook added, "Why don't we wait for the police in the common room? There are plenty of games, some snacks in the fridge, and"—her eyes shifted briefly to Ms. Friedlander—"a large closet where we can lock up Angela."

Once Ms. Friedlander had been locked in the common room closet and everyone else had settled into comfortable chairs, Mrs. Cook took a platter of sandwiches and brownies out of a small refrigerator in the corner of the room.

Offering them to the girls, she explained, "Our cook made these before he left this afternoon. We thought you girls would be hungry when you got back."

The wind whipped through a chink in the windowpane, sending a wild spray of snow onto the sill. The lights went out.

Bess gasped, dropping her brownie on her lap. "I can't stand another minute of darkness!"

Mrs. Cook fumbled her way across the hall to Mr. Moralis's office and returned with a lit candle. She looked at Bess and Lila indulgently. "You poor dears. Being shut away in that awful place. I can't imagine how you must have felt."

Bess relaxed in the candlelight. "But we're okay now," she said, sitting back in her armchair and nibbling on her brownie. "Candlelight and homemade brownies—total luxury. Thank you, Mrs. Cook. And thank you, Nancy. If you weren't such an awesome detective, we'd still be eating soggy graham crackers in that crypt."

"With the Black Cat herself for company," Nancy teased.

At that moment a dark form jumped onto the window sill outside, next to where Nancy sat. Everyone started.

"Tassie!" Lila exclaimed. "Let's bring him in from the storm."

Nancy rose from her chair and gingerly opened the window. The cat rushed inside, skirting everyone and turning down the long hallway that led to the dining room.

"I don't know if you should have suggested that, Lila dear," Mrs. Cook said frowning.

"Why not?" Lila said. "He's probably just going to the kitchen to catch mice. We're lucky to have him."

"Hmm—a black cat who brings good luck," Bess mused. "That's a twist."

"I'll take skill over luck any day. And guess who has tons of that?" Mrs. Cook said.

"Nancy!" George and Bess answered together, grinning at their friend.

**Do your younger brothers and sisters
want to read books like yours?**

**Let them know there
are books just for *them!***

They can join Nancy Drew and her best
friends as they collect clues and solve
mysteries in

THE

NANCY DREW

NOTEBOOKS®

Starting with
#1 The Slumber Party Secret
#2 The Lost Locket
#3 The Secret Santa
#4 Bad Day for Ballet

AND

**Meet up with suspense and mystery
in The Hardy Boys® are: The Clues Brothers™**

Starting with

#1 The Gross Ghost Mystery
#2 The Karate Clue
#3 First Day, Worst Day
#4 Jump Shot Detectives

A MINSTREL® BOOK

Published by Pocket Books

2324